PENGUIN MODERN CLASSICS

YOUTH

and

THE END OF THE TETHER

Joseph Conrad (originally Konrad Korzeniowski) was born in Russian Poland in 1857, and passed his childhood in the shadow of revolution. His parents died when he was quite young. At the age of seventeen he went to Marseilles to become an apprentice in the merchant marine. This began a long period of adventure at sea, Conrad having his share of hardship, shipwreck, and other accidents. He became a British subject in 1886. In 1889, at the age of thirty-one, he came to London for a rest after fifteen years at sea. On this short London holiday he began writing a sea novel, which, after surviving subsequent jungle travel, shipwreck on the Congo, and a railway cloakroom in Berlin, came into the hands of Edward Garnett and through him to a London publisher. The book was *Almayer's Folly*, destined to be the first of a long series of novels and stories, mostly inspired by his experiences of life at sea, which have placed him in the front rank of English literature. He died in 1924.

JOSEPH CONRAD

YOUTH
and
THE END OF THE TETHER

PENGUIN BOOKS

Penguin Books Ltd, Harmondsworth, Middlesex, England
Penguin Books, 625 Madison Avenue, New York, New York 10022, U.S.A.
Penguin Books Australia Ltd, Ringwood, Victoria, Australia
Penguin Books Canada Ltd, 2801 John Street, Markham, Ontario, Canada L3R 1B4
Penguin Books (N.Z.) Ltd, 182–190 Wairau Road, Auckland 10, New Zealand

—

'Youth' first published 1898
'The End of the Tether' first published 1902
Published in Penguin Modern Classics 1975
Reprinted 1976, 1978

—

Made and printed in Great Britain by
Hazell Watson & Viney Ltd,
Aylesbury, Bucks
Set in Linotype Granjon

CONTENTS

TO
My Wife

> ...*but the Dwarf answered:*
> *'No, something human is dearer*
> *to me than the wealth of the world.'*
> — GRIMM'S TALES

YOUTH: A NARRATIVE

THIS could have occurred nowhere but in England, where men and sea interpenetrate, so to speak – the sea entering into the life of most men, and the men knowing something or everything about the sea, in the way of amusement, of travel, or of bread-winning.

We were sitting round a mahogany table that reflected the bottle, the claret-glasses, and our faces as we leaned on our elbows. There was a director of companies, an accountant, a lawyer, Marlow, and myself. The director had been a *Conway* boy, the accountant had served four years at sea, the lawyer – a fine crusted Tory, High Churchman, the best of old fellows, the soul of honour – had been chief officer in the P. & O. service in the good old days when mail-boats were square-rigged at least on two masts, and used to come down the China Sea before a fair monsoon with stun'-sails set alow and aloft. We all began life in the merchant service. Between the five of us there was the strong bond of the sea, and also the fellowship of the craft, which no amount of enthusiasm for yachting, cruising, and so on can give, since one is only the amusement of life and the other is life itself.

Marlow (at least I think that is how he spelt his name) told the story, or rather the chronicle, of a voyage : –

'Yes, I have seen a little of the Eastern seas; but what I remember best is my first voyage there. You fellows know there are those voyages that seem ordered for the illustration of life, that might stand for a symbol of existence. You fight, work, sweat, nearly kill yourself, sometimes do kill yourself, trying to accomplish something – and you can't. Not from any fault of yours. You simply can do nothing, neither great nor little – not a thing in the world – not even marry an old maid, or get a wretched 600-ton cargo of coal to its port of destination.

'It was altogether a memorable affair. It was my first voyage to the East, and my first voyage as second mate; it was also my skipper's first command. You'll admit it was time. He was sixty if a day; a little man, with a broad, not very straight back, with

9

bowed shoulders and one leg more bandy than the other, he had that queer twisted-about appearance you see so often in men who work in the fields. He had a nut-cracker face – chin and nose trying to come together over a sunken mouth – and it was framed in iron-gray fluffy hair, that looked like a chin-strap of cotton-wool sprinkled with coal-dust. And he had blue eyes in that old face of his, which were amazingly like a boy's, with that candid expression some quite common men preserve to the end of their days by a rare internal gift of simplicity of heart and rectitude of soul. What induced him to accept me was a wonder. I had come out of a crack Australian clipper, where I had been third officer, and he seemed to have a prejudice against crack clippers as aristocratic and high-toned. He said to me, "You know, in this ship you will have to work." I said I had to work in every ship I had ever been in. "Ah, but this is different, and you gentlemen out of them big ships; ... but there! I dare say you will do. Join tomorrow."

'I joined tomorrow. It was twenty-two years ago; and I was just twenty. How time passes! It was one of the happiest days of my life. Fancy! Second mate for the first time – a really responsible officer! I wouldn't have thrown up my new billet for a fortune. The mate looked me over carefully. He was also an old chap, but of another stamp. He had a Roman nose, a snow-white, long beard, and his name was Mahon, but he insisted that it should be pronounced Mann. He was well connected; yet there was something wrong with his luck, and he had never got on.

'As to the captain, he had been for years in coasters, then in the Mediterranean, and last in the West Indian trade. He had never been round the Capes. He could just write a kind of sketchy hand, and didn't care for writing at all. Both were thorough good seamen of course, and between those two old chaps I felt like a small boy between two grandfathers.

'The ship also was old. Her name was the *Judea*. Queer name, isn't it? She belonged to a man Wilmer, Wilcox – some name like that; but he has been bankrupt and dead these twenty years or more, and his name don't matter. She had been laid up in Shadwell basin for ever so long. You may imagine her state. She was all rust, dust, grime – soot aloft, dirt on deck. To me it was like coming out of a palace into a ruined cottage. She was about

400 tons, had a primitive windlass, wooden latches to the doors, not a bit of brass about her, and a big square stern. There was on it, below her name in big letters, a lot of scrollwork, with the gilt off, and some sort of a coat of arms, with the motto "Do or Die" underneath. I remember it took my fancy immensely. There was a touch of romance in it, something that made me love the old thing – something that appealed to my youth!

'We left London in ballast – sand ballast – to load a cargo of coal in a northern port for Bankok. Bankok! I thrilled. I had been six years at sea, but had only seen Melbourne and Sydney, very good places, charming places in their way – but Bankok!

'We worked out of the Thames under canvas, with a North Sea pilot on board. His name was Jermyn, and he dodged all day long about the galley drying his handkerchief before the stove. Apparently he never slept. He was a dismal man, with a perpetual tear sparkling at the end of his nose, who either had been in trouble, or was in trouble, or expected to be in trouble – couldn't be happy unless something went wrong. He mistrusted my youth, my common-sense, and my seamanship, and made a point of showing it in a hundred little ways. I dare say he was right. It seems to me I knew very little then, and I know not much more now; but I cherish a hate for that Jermyn to this day.

'We were a week working up as far as Yarmouth Roads, and then we got into a gale – the famous October gale of twenty-two years ago. It was wind, lightning, sleet, snow, and a terrific sea. We were flying light, and you may imagine how bad it was when I tell you we had smashed bulwarks and a flooded deck. On the second night she shifted her ballast into the lee bow, and by that time we had been blown off somewhere on the Dogger Bank. There was nothing for it but to go below with shovels and try to right her, and there we were in that vast hold, gloomy like a cavern, the tallow dips stuck and flickering on the beams, the gale howling above, the ship tossing about like mad on her side; there we all were, Jermyn, the captain, every one, hardly able to keep our feet, engaged on that gravedigger's work, and trying to toss shovelfuls of wet sand up to windward. At every tumble of the ship you could see vaguely in the dim light men falling down with a great flourish of shovels. One of the ship's boys (we had two), impressed by the weirdness of the scene, wept as if his heart would break. We could hear him blubbering somewhere in the shadows.

'On the third day the gale died out, and by-and-by a north-country tug picked us up. We took sixteen days in all to get from London to the Tyne! When we got into dock we had lost our turn for loading, and they hauled us off to a tier where we remained for a month. Mrs Beard (the captain's name was Beard) came from Colchester to see the old man. She lived on board. The crew of runners had left, and there remained only the officers, one boy and the steward, a mulatto who answered to the name of Abraham. Mrs Beard was an old woman, with a face all wrinkled and ruddy like a winter apple, and the figure of a young girl. She caught sight of me once, sewing on a button, and insisted on having my shirts to repair. This was something different from the captains' wives I had known on board crack clippers. When I brought her the shirts, she said: "And the socks? They want mending, I am sure, and John's – Captain Beard's – things are all in order now. I would be glad of something to do." Bless the old woman. She overhauled my outfit for me, and meantime I read for the first time *Sartor Resartus* and Burnaby's *Ride to Khiva*. I didn't understand much of the first then; but I remember I preferred the soldier to the philosopher at the time; a preference which life has only confirmed. One was a man, and the other was either more – or less. However, they are both dead and Mrs Beard is dead, and youth, strength, genius, thoughts, achievements, simple hearts – all dies ... No matter.

'They loaded us at last. We shipped a crew. Eight able seamen and two boys. We hauled off one evening to the buoys at the dock-gates, ready to go out, and with a fair prospect of beginning the voyage next day. Mrs Beard was to start for home by a late train. When the ship was fast we went to tea. We sat rather silent through the meal – Mahon, the old couple, and I. I finished first, and slipped away for a smoke, my cabin being in a deck-house just against the poop. It was high water, blowing fresh with a drizzle; the double dock-gates were opened, and the steam-colliers were going in and out in the darkness with their lights burning bright, a great plashing of propellers, rattling of winches, and a lot of hailing on the pier-heads. I watched the procession of head-lights gliding high and of green lights gliding low in the night, when suddenly a red gleam flashed at me, vanished, came into view again, and remained. The fore-end of a steamer loomed up close. I shouted down the cabin, "Come up, quick!" and then heard a startled voice saying afar in the dark, "Stop her, sir." A bell jingled. Another voice cried warningly, "We are going right into that barque, sir." The answer to this was a gruff "All right," and the next thing was a heavy crash as the steamer struck a glancing blow with the bluff of her bow about our fore-rigging. There was a moment of confusion, yelling, and running about. Steam roared. Then somebody was heard saying, "All clear, sir" . . . "Are you all right?" asked the gruff voice. I had jumped forward to see the damage, and hailed back, "I think so." "Easy astern," said the gruff voice. A bell jingled. "What steamer is that?" screamed Mahon. By that time she was no more to us than a bulky shadow manoeuvring a little way off. They shouted at us some name – a woman's name, Miranda or Melissa – or some such thing. "This means another month in this beastly hole," said Mahon to me, as we peered with lamps about the splintered bulwarks and broken braces. "But where's the captain?"

'We had not heard or seen anything of him all that time. We went aft to look. A doleful voice arose hailing somewhere in the middle of the dock, "*Judea* ahoy!" . . . How the devil did he get there? . . . "Hallo!" we shouted. "I am adrift in our boat without oars," he cried. A belated water-man offered his services, and Mahon struck a bargain with him for half-a-crown to tow our skipper alongside; but it was Mrs Beard that came up the ladder first. They had been floating about the dock in that mizzly cold rain for nearly an hour. I was never so surprised in my life.

'It appears that when he heard my shout "Come up" he understood at once what was the matter, caught up his wife, ran on deck, and across, and down into our boat, which was fast to the ladder. Not bad for a sixty-year-old. Just imagine that old fellow saving heroically in his arms that old woman – the woman of his life. He set her down on a thwart, and was ready to climb back on board when the painter came adrift somehow, and away they went together. Of course in the confusion we did not hear him shouting. He looked abashed. She said cheerfully, "I suppose it does not matter my losing the train now?" "No, Jenny – you go below and get warm," he growled. Then to us: "A sailor has no business with a wife – I say. There I was, out of the ship. Well, no harm done this time. Let's go and look at what that fool of a steamer smashed."

'It wasn't much, but it delayed us three weeks. At the end of that time, the captain being engaged with his agents, I carried Mrs Beard's bag to the railway-station and put her all comfy into a third-class carriage. She lowered the window to say, "You are a good young man. If you see John – Captain Beard – without his muffler at night, just remind him from me to keep his throat well wrapped up." "Certainly, Mrs Beard," I said. "You are a good young man; I noticed how attentive you are to John – to Captain –" The train pulled out suddenly; I took my cap off to the old woman: I never saw her again . . . Pass the bottle.

'We went to sea next day. When we made that start for Bankok we had been already three months out of London. We had expected to be a fortnight or so – at the outside.

'It was January, and the weather was beautiful – the beautiful sunny winter weather that has more charm than in the summertime, because it is unexpected, and crisp, and you know it won't, it can't, last long. It's like a windfall, like a godsend, like an unexpected piece of luck.

'It lasted all down the North Sea, all down Channel; and it lasted till we were three hundred miles or so to the westward of the Lizards: then the wind went round to the sou'west and began to pipe up. In two days it blew a gale. The *Judea*, hove to, wallowed on the Atlantic like an old candle-box. It blew day after day: it blew with spite, without interval, without mercy, without rest. The world was nothing but an immensity of great foaming waves rushing at us, under a sky low enough to touch with the hand and dirty like a smoked ceiling. In the stormy space surrounding us there was as much flying spray as air. Day after day and night after night there was nothing round the ship but the howl of the wind, the tumult of the sea, the noise of water pouring over her deck. There was no rest for her and no rest for us. She tossed, she pitched, she stood on her head, she sat on her tail, she rolled, she groaned, and we had to hold on while on deck and cling to our bunks when below, in a constant effort of body and worry of mind.

'One night Mahon spoke through the small window of my berth. It opened right into my very bed, and I was lying there sleepless, in my boots, feeling as though I had not slept for years, and could not if I tried. He said excitedly –

' "You got the sounding-rod in here, Marlow? I can't get the pumps to suck. By God! it's no child's play."

'I gave him the sounding-rod and lay down again, trying to think of various things – but I thought only of the pumps. When I came on deck they were still at it, and my watch relieved at the pumps. By the light of the lantern brought on deck to examine the sounding-rod I caught a glimpse of their weary, serious faces. We pumped all the four hours. We pumped all night, all day, all the week – watch and watch. She was working herself loose, and leaked badly – not enough to drown us at once, but enough to kill us with the work at the pumps. And while we pumped the ship was going from us piecemeal: the bulwarks went, the stanchions were torn out, the ventilators smashed, the cabin-door burst in. There was not a dry spot in the ship. She was being gutted bit by bit. The long-boat changed, as if by magic, into matchwood where she stood in her gripes. I had lashed her myself, and was rather proud of my handiwork, which had withstood so long the malice of the sea. And we pumped. And there was no break in the weather. The sea was white like a sheet of foam, like a caldron of boiling milk; there was not a break in the clouds, no – not the size of a man's hand – no, not for so much as ten seconds. There was for us no sky, there were for us no stars, no sun, no universe – nothing but angry clouds and an infuriated sea. We pumped watch and watch, for dear life; and it seemed to last for months, for years, for all eternity, as though we had been dead and gone to a hell for sailors. We forgot the day of the week, the name of the month, what year it was, and whether we had ever been ashore. The sails blew away, she lay broadside on under a weather-cloth, the ocean poured over her, and we did not care. We turned those handles, and had the eyes of idiots. As soon as we had crawled on deck I used to take a round turn with a rope about the men, the pumps, and the mainmast, and we turned, we turned incessantly, with the water to our waists, to our necks, over our heads. It was all one. We had forgotten how it felt to be dry.

'And there was somewhere in me the thought: By Jove! this is the deuce of an adventure – something you read about; and it is my first voyage as second mate – and I am only twenty – and here I am lasting it out as well as any of these men, and keeping my chaps up to the mark. I was pleased. I would not have given up the experience for worlds. I had moments of exultation. Whenever the old dismantled craft pitched heavily with her counter high in the air, she seemed to me to throw up, like an appeal, like a defiance, like a cry to the clouds without mercy, the words written on her stern: "*Judea*, London. Do or Die."

'O youth! The strength of it, the faith of it, the imagination of it! To me she was not an old rattle-trap carting about the world a lot of coal for a freight – to me she was the endeavour, the test, the trial of life. I think of her with pleasure, with affection, with regret – as you would think of someone dead you have loved. I shall never forget her . . . Pass the bottle.

'One night when tied to the mast, as I explained, we were pumping on, deafened with the wind, and without spirit enough in us to wish ourselves dead, a heavy sea crashed aboard and swept clean over us. As soon as I got my breath I shouted, as in duty bound, "Keep on, boys!" when suddenly I felt something hard floating on deck strike the calf of my leg. I made a grab at it and missed. It was so dark we could not see each other's faces within a foot – you understand.

'After that thump the ship kept quiet for a while, and the thing, whatever it was, struck my leg again. This time I caught it – and it was a saucepan. At first, being stupid with fatigue and thinking of nothing but the pumps, I did not understand what I had in my hand. Suddenly it dawned upon me, and I shouted, "Boys, the house on deck is gone. Leave this, and let's look for the cook."

'There was a deck-house forward, which contained the galley, the cook's berth, and the quarters of the crew. As we had expected for days to see it swept away, the hands had been ordered to sleep in the cabin – the only safe place in the ship. The steward, Abraham, however, persisted in clinging to his berth, stupidly, like a mule – from sheer fright I believe, like an animal that won't leave a stable falling in an earthquake. So we went to look for him. It was chancing death, since once out of our lashings we were as exposed as if on a raft. But we went. The house was shattered as if a shell had exploded inside. Most of it had gone overboard – stove, men's quarters, and their property, all was gone; but two posts, holding a portion of the bulkhead to which Abraham's bunk was attached, remained as if by a miracle. We groped in the ruins and came upon this, and there he was, sitting in his bunk, surrounded by foam and wreckage, jabbering cheerfully to himself. He was out of his mind; completely and for ever mad, with this sudden shock coming upon the fag-end of his endurance. We snatched him up, lugged him aft, and pitched him head-first down the cabin companion. You understand there was no time to carry him down with infinite precautions and wait to see how he got on. Those below would pick him up at the bottom of the stairs all right. We were in a hurry to go back to the pumps. That business could not wait. A bad leak is an inhuman thing.

'One would think that the sole purpose of that fiendish gale had been to make a lunatic of that poor devil of a mulatto. It eased before morning, and next day the sky cleared, and as the sea went down the leak took up. When it came to bending a fresh set of sails the crew demanded to put back – and really there was nothing else to do. Boats gone, decks swept clean, cabin gutted, men without a stitch but what they stood in, stores spoiled, ship strained. We put her head for home, and – would you believe it? The wind came east right in our teeth. It blew fresh, it blew continuously. We had to beat up every inch of the way, but she did not leak so badly, the water keeping comparatively smooth. Two hours' pumping in every four is no joke – but it kept her afloat as far as Falmouth.

'The good people there live on casualties of the sea, and no doubt were glad to see us. A hungry crowd of shipwrights sharpened their chisels at the sight of that carcass of a ship. And, by Jove! they had pretty pickings off us before they were done. I fancy the owner was already in a tight place. There were delays. Then it was decided to take part of the cargo out and caulk her topsides. This was done, the repairs finished, cargo reshipped; a new crew came on board, and we went out – for Bankok. At the end of a week we were back again. The crew said they weren't going to Bankok – a hundred and fifty days' passage – in a something hooker that wanted pumping eight hours out of the twenty-four; and the nautical papers inserted again the little paragraph: *"Judea.* Barque. Tyne to Bankok; coals; put back to Falmouth leaky and with crew refusing duty."

'There were more delays – more tinkering. The owner came down for a day, and said she was as right as a little fiddle. Poor old Captain Beard looked like the ghost of a Geordie skipper – through the worry and humiliation of it. Remember he was sixty, and it was his first command. Mahon said it was a foolish business, and would end badly. I loved the ship more than ever, and wanted awfully to get to Bankok. To Bankok! Magic name, blessed name. Mesopotamia wasn't a patch on it. Remember I was twenty, and it was my first second-mate's billet, and the East was waiting for me.

'We went out and anchored in the outer roads with a fresh crew – the third. She leaked worse than ever. It was as if those confounded shipwrights had actually made a hole in her. This time we did not even go outside. The crew simply refused to man the windlass.

'They towed us back to the inner harbour, and we became a fixture, a feature, an institution of the place. People pointed us out to visitors as "That 'ere barque that's going to Bankok – has been here six months – put back three times." On holidays the small boys pulling about in boats would hail, *"Judea,* ahoy!" and if a head showed above the rail shouted, "Where you bound to? – Bankok?" and jeered. We were only three on board. The poor old skipper mooned in the cabin. Mahon undertook the cooking, and unexpectedly developed all a Frenchman's genius for preparing nice little messes. I looked languidly after the rigging. We became citizens of Falmouth. Every shopkeeper knew us. At the barber's or tobacconist's they asked familiarly, "Do you think you will ever get to Bankok?" Meantime the owner, the underwriters, and the charterers squabbled amongst themselves in London, and our pay went on . . . Pass the bottle.

'It was horrid. Morally it was worse than pumping for life. It seemed as though we had been forgotten by the world, belonged to nobody, would get nowhere; it seemed that, as if be-witched, we would have to live for ever and ever in that inner harbour, a derision and a by-word to generations of long-shore loafers and dishonest boatmen. I obtained three months' pay and a five days' leave, and made a rush for London. It took me a day to get there and pretty well another to come back – but three months' pay went all the same. I don't know what I did with it. I went to a music-hall, I believe, lunched, dined, and supped in a swell place in Regent Street, and was back to time, with nothing but a complete set of Byron's works and a new railway rug to show for three months' work. The boat-man who pulled me off to the ship said: "Hallo! I thought you had left the old thing. *She* will never get to Bankok." "That's all *you* know about it," I said, scornfully – but I didn't like that prophecy at all.

'Suddenly a man, some kind of agent to somebody, appeared with full powers. He had grog-blossoms all over his face, an in-domitable energy, and was a jolly soul. We leaped into life again. A hulk came alongside, took our cargo, and then we went into dry dock to get our copper stripped. No wonder she leaked. The poor thing, strained beyond endurance by the gale, had, as if in disgust, spat out all the oakum of her lower seams. She was recaulked, new coppered, and made as tight as a bottle. We went back to the hulk and reshipped our cargo.

'Then, on a fine moonlight night, all the rats left the ship.

'We had been infested with them. They had destroyed our sails, consumed more stores than the crew, affably shared our beds and our dangers, and now, when the ship was made sea-worthy, concluded to clear out. I called Mahon to enjoy the spectacle. Rat after rat appeared on our rail, took a last look over his shoulder, and leaped with a hollow thud into the empty hulk. We tried to count them, but soon lost the tale. Mahon said: "Well, well! don't talk to me about the intelligence of rats. They ought to have left before, when we had that narrow squeak from foundering. There you have the proof how silly is the supersti-tion about them. They leave a good ship for an old rotten hulk, where there is nothing to eat, too, the fools! ... I don't believe they know what is safe or what is good for them, any more than you or I."

'And after some more talk we agreed that the wisdom of rats

had been grossly overrated, being in fact no greater than that of men.

'The story of the ship was known, by this, all up the Channel from Land's End to the Forelands, and we could get no crew on the south coast. They sent us one all complete from Liverpool, and we left once more – for Bankok.

'We had fair breezes, smooth water right into the tropics, and the old *Judea* lumbered along in the sunshine. When she went eight knots everything cracked aloft, and we tied our caps to our heads; but mostly she strolled on at the rate of three miles an hour. What could you expect? She was tired – that old ship. Her youth was where mine is – where yours is – you fellows who listen to this yarn; and what friend would throw your years and your weariness in your face? We didn't grumble at her. To us aft, at least, it seemed as though we had been born in her, reared in her, had lived in her for ages, had never known any other ship. I would just as soon have abused the old village church at home for not being a cathedral.

'And for me there was also my youth to make me patient. There was all the East before me, and all life, and the thought that I had been tried in that ship and had come out pretty well. And I thought of men of old who, centuries ago, went that road in ships that sailed no better, to the land of palms, and spices, and yellow sands, and of brown nations ruled by kings more cruel than Nero the Roman, and more splendid than Solomon the Jew. The old bark lumbered on, heavy with her age and the burden of her cargo, while I lived the life of youth in ignorance and hope. She lumbered on through an interminable procession of days; and the fresh gilding flashed back at the setting sun, seemed to cry out over the darkening sea the words painted on her stern, "*Judea*, London. Do or Die."

'Then we entered the Indian Ocean and steered northerly for Java Head. The winds were light. Weeks slipped by. She crawled on, do or die, and people at home began to think of posting us as overdue.

'One Saturday evening, I being off duty, the men asked me to give them an extra bucket of water or so – for washing clothes. As I did not wish to screw on the fresh-water pump so late, I went forward whistling, and with a key in my hand to unlock the forepeak scuttle, intending to serve the water out of a spare tank we kept there.

'The smell down below was as unexpected as it was frightful. One would have thought hundreds of paraffin-lamps had been flaring and smoking in that hole for days. I was glad to get out. The man with me coughed and said, "Funny smell, sir." I answered negligently, "It's good for the health they say," and walked aft.

'The first thing I did was to put my head down the square of the midship ventilator. As I lifted the lid a visible breath, something like a thin fog, a puff of faint haze, rose from the opening. The ascending air was hot, and had a heavy, sooty, paraffiny smell. I gave one sniff, and put down the lid gently. It was no use choking myself. The cargo was on fire.

'Next day she began to smoke in earnest. You see it was to be expected, for though the coal was of a safe kind, that cargo had been so handled, so broken up with handling, that it looked more like smithy coal than anything else. Then it had been wetted – more than once. It rained all the time we were taking it back from the hulk, and now with this long passage it got heated, and there was another case of spontaneous combustion.

'The captain called us into the cabin. He had a chart spread on the table, and looked unhappy. He said, "The coast of West Australia is near, but I mean to proceed to our destination. It is the hurricane month, too; but we will just keep her head for Bankok, and fight the fire. No more putting back anywhere, if we all get roasted. We will try first to stifle this 'ere damned combustion by want of air."

'We tried. We battened down everything, and still she smoked. The smoke kept coming out through imperceptible crevices; it forced itself through bulkheads and covers; it oozed here and there and everywhere in slender threads, in an invisible film, in an incomprehensible manner. It made its way into the cabin, into the forecastle; it poisoned the sheltered places on the deck, it could be sniffed as high as the mainyard. It was clear that if the smoke came out the air came in. This was disheartening. This combustion refused to be stifled.

'We resolved to try water, and took the hatches off. Enormous volumes of smoke, whitish, yellowish, thick, greasy, misty, choking, ascended as high as the trucks. All hands cleared out aft. Then the poisonous cloud blew away, and we went back to work in a smoke that was no thicker now than that of an ordinary factory chimney.

'We rigged the force-pump, got the hose along, and by-and-by it burst. Well, it was as old as the ship – a prehistoric hose, and past repair. Then we pumped with the feeble head-pump, drew water with buckets, and in this way managed in time to pour lots of Indian Ocean into the main hatch. The bright stream flashed in sunshine, fell into a layer of white crawling smoke, and vanished on the black surface of coal. Steam ascended mingling with the smoke. We poured salt water as into a barrel without a bottom. It was our fate to pump in that ship, to pump out of her, to pump into her; and after keeping water out of her to save ourselves from being drowned, we frantically poured water into her to save ourselves from being burnt.

'And she crawled on, do or die, in the serene weather. The sky was a miracle of purity, a miracle of azure. The sea was polished, was blue, was pellucid, was sparkling like a precious stone, extending on all sides, all round to the horizon – as if the whole terrestrial globe had been one jewel, one colossal sapphire, a single gem fashioned into a planet. And on the lustre of the great calm waters the *Judea* glided imperceptibly, enveloped in languid and unclean vapours, in a lazy cloud that drifted to lee-ward, light and slow; a pestiferous cloud defiling the splendour of sea and sky.

'All this time of course we saw no fire. The cargo smouldered at the bottom somewhere. Once Mahon, as we were working side by side, said to me with a queer smile: "Now, if she only would spring a tidy leak – like that time when we first left the Channel – it would put a stopper on this fire. Wouldn't it?" I remarked irrelevantly, "Do you remember the rats?"

'We fought the fire and sailed the ship too as carefully as though nothing had been the matter. The steward cooked and attended on us. Of the other twelve men, eight worked while four rested. Everyone took his turn, captain included. There was equality, and if not exactly fraternity, then a deal of good feeling. Sometimes a man, as he dashed a bucketful of water down the hatchway, would yell out, "Hurrah for Bankok!" and the rest laughed. But generally we were taciturn and serious – and thirsty. Oh! how thirsty! And we had to be careful with the water. Strict allowance. The ship smoked, the sun blazed ... Pass the bottle.

'We tried everything. We even made an attempt to dig down to the fire. No good, of course. No man could remain more than a minute below. Mahon, who went first, fainted there, and the man who went to fetch him out did likewise. We lugged them out on deck. Then I leaped down to show how easily it could be done. They had learned wisdom by that time, and contented themselves by fishing for me with a chain-hook tied to a broom-handle, I believe. I did not offer to go and fetch up my shovel, which was left down below.

'Things began to look bad. We put the long boat into the water. The second boat was ready to swing out. We had also another, a 14-foot thing on davits aft, where it was quite safe.

'Then, behold, the smoke suddenly decreased. We redoubled our efforts to flood the bottom of the ship. In two days there was no smoke at all. Everybody was on the broad grin. This was on a Friday. On Saturday no work, but sailing the ship of course, was done. The men washed their clothes and their faces for the first time in a fortnight, and had a special dinner given them. They spoke of spontaneous combustion with contempt, and implied *they* were the boys to put out combustions. Somehow we all felt as though we each had inherited a large fortune. But a beastly smell of burning hung about the ship. Captain Beard had hollow eyes and sunken cheeks. I had never noticed so much before how twisted and bowed he was. He and Mahon prowled soberly about hatches and ventilators, sniffing. It struck me suddenly poor Mahon was a very, very old chap. As to me, I was as pleased and proud as though I had helped to win a great naval battle. O! Youth!

'The night was fine. In the morning a homeward-bound ship passed us hull down – the first we had seen for months; but we were nearing the land at last, Java Head being about 190 miles off, and nearly due north.

'Next day it was my watch on deck from eight to twelve. At breakfast the captain observed, "It's wonderful how that smell hangs about the cabin." About ten, the mate being on the poop, I stepped down on the main-deck for a moment. The carpenter's bench stood abaft the mainmast: I leaned against it sucking at my pipe, and the carpenter, a young chap, came to talk to me. He remarked, "I think we have done very well, haven't we?" and then I perceived with annoyance the fool was trying to tilt the bench. I said curtly, "Don't, Chips," and immediately became aware of a queer sensation, of an absurd delusion, – I seemed somehow to be in the air. I heard all round me like a pent-up breath released – as if a thousand giants simultaneously had said Phoo! – and felt a dull concussion which made my ribs ache suddenly. No doubt about it – I was in the air, and my body was describing a short parabola. But short as it was, I had the time to think several thoughts in, as far as I can remember, the following order: "This can't be the carpenter – What is it? – Some accident – Submarine volcano? – Coals, gas! – By Jove! we are being blown up – Everybody's dead – I am falling into the after-hatch – I see fire in it."

'The coal-dust suspended in the air of the hold had glowed dull-red at the moment of the explosion. In the twinkling of an eye, in an infinitesimal fraction of a second since the first tilt of the bench, I was sprawling full length on the cargo. I picked myself up and scrambled out. It was quick like a rebound. The deck was a wilderness of smashed timber, lying crosswise like trees in a wood after a hurricane; an immense curtain of soiled rags waved gently before me – it was the main-sail blown to strips. I thought, The masts will be toppling over directly; and to get out of the way bolted on all-fours towards the poop-ladder. The first person I saw was Mahon, with eyes like saucers, his mouth open, and the long white hair standing straight on end round his head like a silver halo. He was just about to go down when the sight of the main-deck stirring, heaving up, and changing into splinters before his eyes, petrified him on the top step. I stared at him in unbelief, and he stared at me with a queer kind of shocked curiosity. I did not know that I had no hair, no eyebrows, no eyelashes, that my young moustache was burnt off, that my face was black, one cheek laid open, my nose cut, and my chin bleeding. I had lost my cap, one of my slippers, and my shirt was torn to rags. Of all this I was not aware. I was amazed to see the ship still afloat, the poop-deck whole – and, most of all, to see anybody alive. Also the peace of the sky and the serenity of the sea were distinctly surprising. I suppose I expected to see them convulsed with horror . . . Pass the bottle.

'There was a voice hailing the ship from somewhere – in the air, in the sky – I couldn't tell. Presently I saw the captain – and he was mad. He asked me eagerly, "Where's the cabin-table?" and to hear such a question was a frightful shock. I had just been blown up, you understand, and vibrated with that experience, – I wasn't quite sure whether I was alive. Mahon began to stamp with both feet and yelled at him, "Good God! don't you see the deck's blown out of her?" I found my voice, and stammered out as if conscious of some gross neglect of duty, "I don't know where the cabin-table is." It was like an absurd dream.

'Do you know what he wanted next? Well, he wanted to trim the yards. Very placidly, and as if lost in thought, he insisted on having the foreyard squared. "I don't know if there's anybody alive," said Mahon, almost tearfully. "Surely," he said, gently, "there will be enough left to square the foreyard."

'The old chap, it seems, was in his own berth winding up the chronometers, when the shock sent him spinning. Immediately it occurred to him – as he said afterwards – that the ship had struck something, and ran out into the cabin. There, he saw, the cabin-table had vanished somewhere. The deck being blown up, it had fallen down into the lazarette of course. Where we had our breakfast that morning he saw only a great hole in the floor. This appeared to him so awfully mysterious, and impressed him so immensely, that what he saw and heard after he got on deck were mere trifles in comparison. And, mark, he noticed directly the wheel deserted and his barque off her course – and his only thought was to get that miserable, stripped, undecked, smouldering shell of a ship back again with her head pointing at her port of destination. Bankok! That's what he was after. I tell you this quiet, bowed, bandy-legged, almost deformed little man was immense in the singleness of his idea and in his placid ignorance of our agitation. He motioned us forward with a commanding gesture, and went to take the wheel himself.

'Yes; that was the first thing we did – trim the yards of that wreck! No one was killed, or even disabled, but everyone was more or less hurt. You should have seen them! Some were in rags, with black faces, like coalheavers, like sweeps, and had bullet heads that seemed closely cropped, but were in fact singed to the skin. Others of the watch below, awakened by being shot out from their collapsing bunks, shivered incessantly, and kept on groaning even as we went about our work. But they all worked. That crew of Liverpool hard cases had in them the right stuff. It's my experience they always have. It is the sea that gives it – the vastness, the loneliness surrounding their dark stolid souls. Ah! Well! we stumbled, we crept, we fell, we barked our shins on the wreckage, we hauled. The masts stood, but we did not know how much they might be charred down below. It was nearly calm, but a long swell ran from the west and made her roll. They might go at any moment. We looked at them with apprehension. One could not foresee which way they would fall.

'Then we retreated aft and looked about us. The deck was a tangle of planks on edge, of planks on end, of splinters, of ruined woodwork. The masts rose from that chaos like big trees above a matted undergrowth. The interstices of that mass of wreckage were full of something whitish, sluggish, stirring – of something that was like a greasy fog. The smoke of the invisible fire was coming up again, was trailing, like a poisonous thick mist in some valley choked with dead wood. Already lazy wisps were beginning to curl upwards amongst the mass of splinters. Here and there a piece of timber, stuck upright, resembled a post. Half of a fife-rail had been shot through the foresail, and the sky made a patch of glorious blue in the ignobly soiled canvas. A portion of several boards holding together had fallen across the rail, and one end protruded overboard, like a gangway leading upon nothing, like a gangway leading over the deep sea, leading to death – as if inviting us to walk the plank at once and be done with our ridiculous troubles. And still the air, the sky – a ghost, something invisible was hailing the ship.

'Someone had the sense to look over, and there was the helmsman, who had impulsively jumped overboard, anxious to come back. He yelled and swam lustily like a merman, keeping up with the ship. We threw him a rope, and presently he stood amongst us streaming with water and very crestfallen. The captain had surrendered the wheel, and apart, elbow on rail and chin in hand, gazed at the sea wistfully. We asked ourselves, What next? I thought, Now, this is something like. This is great. I wonder what will happen. O youth !

'Suddenly Mahon sighted a steamer far astern. Captain Beard said, "We may do something with her yet." We hoisted two flags, which said in the international language of the sea, "On fire. Want immediate assistance." The steamer grew bigger rapidly, and by-and-by spoke with two flags on her foremast, "I am coming to your assistance."

'In half an hour she was abreast, to windward, within hail, and rolling slightly, with her engines stopped. We lost our composure, and yelled all together with excitement, "We've been blown up." A man in a white helmet, on the bridge, cried "Yes! All right! all right!" and he nodded his head, and smiled, and made soothing motions with his hand as though at a lot of frightened children. One of the boats dropped in the water, and walked towards us upon the sea with her long oars. Four Calashes pulled a swinging stroke. This was my first sight of Malay seamen. I've known them since, but what struck me then was their unconcern: they came alongside, and even the bowman standing up and holding to our main-chains with the boathook did not deign to lift his head for a glance. I thought people who had been blown up deserved more attention.

'A little man, dry like a chip and agile like a monkey, clambered up. It was the mate of the steamer. He gave one look, and cried, "O boys – you had better quit."

'We were silent. He talked apart with the captain for a time, – seemed to argue with him. Then they went away together to the steamer.

'When our skipper came back we learned that the steamer was the *Somerville*, Captain Nash, from West Australia to Singapore *via* Batavia with mails, and that the agreement was she should tow us to Anjer or Batavia, if possible, where we could extinguish the fire by scuttling, and then proceed on our voyage – to Bankok ! The old man seemed excited. "We will do it yet," he said to Mahon, fiercely. He shook his fist at the sky. Nobody else said a word.

'At noon the steamer began to tow. She went ahead slim and high, and what was left of the *Judea* followed at the end of seventy fathom of tow-rope, – followed her swiftly like a cloud of smoke with mast-heads protruding above. We went aloft to furl the sails. We coughed on the yards, and were careful about the bunts. Do you see the lot of us there, putting a neat furl on the sails of that ship doomed to arrive nowhere? There was not a man who didn't think that at any moment the masts would topple over. From aloft we could not see the ship for smoke, and they worked carefully, passing the gaskets with even turns. "Harbour furl – aloft there !" cried Mahon from below.

'You understand this? I don't think one of those chaps expected to get down in the usual way. When we did I heard them saying to each other, "Well, I thought we would come down overboard, in a lump – sticks and all – blame me if I didn't." "That's what I was thinking to myself," would answer wearily another battered and bandaged scarecrow. And, mind, these were men without the drilled-in habit of obedience. To an on-looker they would be a lot of profane scallywags without a re-deeming point. What made them do it – what made them obey me when I, thinking consciously how fine it was, made them drop the bunt of the foresail twice to try and do it better? What? They had no professional reputation – no examples, no praise. It wasn't a sense of duty; they all knew well enough how to shirk, and laze, and dodge – when they had a mind to it – and mostly they had. Was it the two pounds ten a-month that sent them there? They didn't think their pay half good enough. No; it was something in them, something inborn and subtle and ever-lasting. I don't say positively that the crew of a French or German merchantman wouldn't have done it, but I doubt whether it would have been done in the same way. There was a complete-ness in it, something solid like a principle, and masterful like an instinct – a disclosure of something secret – of that hidden some-thing, that gift of good or evil that makes racial difference, that shapes the fate of nations.

'It was that night at ten that, for the first time since we had been fighting it, we saw the fire. The speed of the towing had fanned the smouldering destruction. A blue gleam appeared forward, shining below the wreck of the deck. It wavered in patches, it seemed to stir and creep like the light of a glowworm. I saw it first, and told Mahon. "Then the game's up," he said. "We had better stop this towing, or she will burst out suddenly fore and aft before we can clear out." We set up a yell; rang bells to attract their attention; they towed on. At last Mahon and I had to crawl forward and cut the rope with an axe. There was no time to cast off the lashings. Red tongues could be seen licking the wilderness of splinters under our feet as we made our way back to the poop.

'Of course they very soon found out in the steamer that the rope was gone. She gave a loud blast of her whistle, her lights were seen sweeping in a wide circle, she came up ranging close along-side, and stopped. We were all in a tight group on the poop looking at her. Every man had saved a little bundle or a bag. Suddenly a conical flame with a twisted top shot up forward and threw upon the black sea a circle of light, with the two vessels side by side and heaving gently in its centre. Captain Beard had been sitting on the gratings still and mute for hours, but now he rose slowly and advanced in front of us, to the mizzen-shrouds. Captain Nash hailed: "Come along! Look sharp. I have mail-bags on board. I will take you and your boats to Singapore."

' "Thank you! No!" said our skipper. "We must see the last of the ship."

' "I can't stand by any longer," shouted the other. "Mails — you know."

' "Ay! ay! We are all right."

' "Very well! I'll report you in Singapore . . . Good-bye!"

'He waved his hand. Our men dropped their bundles quietly. The steamer moved ahead, and passing out of the circle of light, vanished at once from our sight, dazzled by the fire which burned fiercely. And then I knew that I would see the East first as commander of a small boat. I thought it fine; and the fidelity to the old ship was fine. We should see the last of her. Oh, the glamour of youth! Oh, the fire of it, more dazzling than the flames of the burning ship, throwing a magic light on the wide earth, leaping audaciously to the sky, presently to be quenched by time, more cruel, more pitiless, more bitter than the sea —

and like the flames of the burning ship surrounded by an impenetrable night.

*

'The old man warned us in his gentle and inflexible way that it was part of our duty to save for the underwriters as much as we could of the ship's gear. Accordingly we went to work aft, while she blazed forward to give us plenty of light. We lugged out a lot of rubbish. What didn't we save? An old barometer fixed with an absurd quantity of screws nearly cost me my life: a sudden rush of smoke came upon me, and I just got away in time. There were various stores, bolts of canvas, coils of rope; the poop looked like a marine bazaar, and the boats were lumbered to the gunwales. One would have thought the old man wanted to take as much as he could of his first command with him. He was very, very quiet, but off his balance evidently. Would you believe it? He wanted to take a length of old stream-cable and a kedge-anchor with him in the long-boat. We said, "Ay, ay, sir," deferentially, and on the quiet let the things slip overboard. The heavy medicine-chest went that way, two bags of green coffee, tins of paint – fancy, paint! – a whole lot of things. Then I was ordered with two hands into the boats to make a stowage and get them ready against the time it would be proper for us to leave the ship.

'We put everything straight, stepped the long-boat's mast for our skipper, who was to take charge of her, and I was not sorry to sit down for a moment. My face felt raw, every limb ached as if broken, I was aware of all my ribs, and would have sworn to a twist in the backbone. The boats, fast astern, lay in a deep shadow, and all around I could see the circle of the sea lighted by the fire. A gigantic flame arose forward straight and clear. It flared fierce, with noises like the whirr of wings, with rumbles as of thunder. There were cracks, detonations, and from the cone of flame the sparks flew upwards, as man is born to trouble, to leaky ships, and to ships that burn.

'What bothered me was that the ship, lying broadside to the swell and to such wind as there was – a mere breath – the boats would not keep astern where they were safe, but persisted, in a pig-headed way boats have, in getting under the counter and then swinging alongside. They were knocking about dangerously and coming near the flame, while the ship rolled on them, and, of course, there was always the danger of the masts going over the side at any moment. I and my two boat-keepers kept them off as best we could, with oars and boat-hooks; but to be constantly at it became exasperating, since there was no reason why we should not leave at once. We could not see those on board, nor could we imagine what caused the delay. The boat-keepers were swearing feebly, and I had not only my share of the work but also had to keep at it two men who showed a constant inclination to lay themselves down and let things slide.

'At last I hailed, "On deck there," and someone looked over. "We're ready here," I said. The head disappeared, and very soon popped up again. "The captain says, All right, sir, and to keep the boats well clear of the ship."

'Half an hour passed. Suddenly there was a frightful racket, rattle, clanking of chain, hiss of water, and millions of sparks flew up into the shivering column of smoke that stood leaning slightly above the ship. The cat-heads had burned away, and the two red-hot anchors had gone to the bottom, tearing out after them two hundred fathom of red-hot chain. The ship trembled, the mass of flame swayed as if ready to collapse, and the fore top-gallant-mast fell. It darted down like an arrow of fire, shot under, and instantly leaping up within an oar's-length of the boats, floated quietly, very black on the luminous sea. I hailed the deck again. After some time a man in an unexpectedly cheerful but also muffled tone, as though he had been trying to speak with his mouth shut, informed me, "Coming directly, sir," and vanished. For a long time I heard nothing but the whirr and roar of the fire. There were also whistling sounds. The boats jumped, tugged at the painters, ran at each other playfully, knocked their sides together, or, do what we would, swung in a bunch against the ship's side. I couldn't stand it any longer, and swarming up a rope, clambered aboard over the stern.

'It was as bright as day. Coming up like this, the sheet of fire facing me was a terrifying sight, and the heat seemed hardly bearable at first. On a settee cushion dragged out of the cabin Captain Beard, his legs drawn up and one arm under his head, slept with the light playing on him. Do you know what the rest were busy about? They were sitting on deck right aft, round an open case, eating bread and cheese and drinking bottled stout.

'On the background of flames twisting in fierce tongues above their heads they seemed at home like salamanders, and looked like a band of desperate pirates. The fire sparkled in the whites of their eyes, gleamed on patches of white skin seen through the torn shirts. Each had the marks as of a battle about him – bandaged heads, tied-up arms, a strip of dirty rag round a knee – and each man had a bottle between his legs and a chunk of cheese in his hand. Mahon got up. With his handsome and disreputable head, his hooked profile, his long white beard, and with an uncorked bottle in his hand, he resembled one of those reckless sea-robbers of old making merry amidst violence and disaster. "The last meal on board," he explained solemnly. "We had nothing to eat all day, and it was no use leaving all this." He flourished the bottle and indicated the sleeping skipper. "He said he couldn't swallow anything, so I got him to lie down," he went on; and as I stared, "I don't know whether you are aware, young fellow, the man had no sleep to speak of for days – and there will be dam' little sleep in the boats." "There will be no boats by-and-by if you fool about much longer," I said, indignantly. I walked up to the skipper and shook him by the shoulder. At last he opened his eyes, but did not move. "Time to leave her, sir," I said quietly.

'He got up painfully, looked at the flames, at the sea sparkling round the ship, and black, black as ink farther away; he looked at the stars shining dim through a thin veil of smoke in a sky black, black as Erebus.

' "Youngest first," he said.

'And the ordinary seaman, wiping his mouth with the back of his hand, got up, clambered over the taffrail, and vanished. Others followed. One, on the point of going over, stopped short to drain his bottle, and with a great swing of his arm flung it at the fire. "Take this!" he cried.

'The skipper lingered disconsolately, and we left him to commune for a while with his first command. Then I went up again and brought him away at last. It was time. The ironwork on the poop was hot to the touch.

'Then the painter of the long-boat was cut, and the three

boats, tied together, drifted clear of the ship. It was just sixteen hours after the explosion when we abandoned her. Mahon had charge of the second boat, and I had the smallest — the 14-foot thing. The long-boat would have taken the lot of us; but the skipper said we must save as much property as we could — for the underwriters — and so I got my first command. I had two men with me, a bag of biscuits, a few tins of meat, and a breaker of water. I was ordered to keep close to the long-boat, that in case of bad weather we might be taken into her.

'And do you know what I thought? I thought I would part company as soon as I could. I wanted to have my first command all to myself. I wasn't going to sail in a squadron if there were a chance of independent cruising. I would make land by myself. I would beat the other boats. Youth! All youth! The silly, charming, beautiful youth.

'But we did not make a start at once. We must see the last of the ship. And so the boats drifted about that night, heaving and setting on the swell. The men dozed, waked, sighed, groaned. I looked at the burning ship.

'Between the darkness of earth and heaven she was burning fiercely upon a disc of purple sea shot by the blood-red play of gleams; upon a disc of water glittering and sinister. A high, clear flame, an immense and lonely flame, ascended from the ocean, and from its summit the black smoke poured continuously at the sky. She burned furiously; mournful and imposing like a funeral pile kindled in the night, surrounded by the sea, watched over by the stars. A magnificent death had come like a grace, like a gift, like a reward to that old ship at the end of her laborious days. The surrender of her weary ghost to the keeping of stars and sea was stirring like the sight of a glorious triumph. The masts fell just before daybreak, and for a moment there was a burst and turmoil of sparks that seemed to fill with flying fire the night patient and watchful, the vast night lying silent upon the sea. At daylight she was only a charred shell, floating still under a cloud of smoke and bearing a glowing mass of coal within.

'Then the oars were got out, and the boats forming in a line moved round her remains as if in procession — the long-boat leading. As we pulled across her stern a slim dart of fire shot out viciously at us, and suddenly she went down, head first, in a great hiss of steam. The unconsumed stern was the last to sink; but the paint had gone, had cracked, had peeled off, and there were no letters, there was no word, no stubborn device that was like her soul, to flash at the rising sun her creed and her name.

'We made our way north. A breeze sprang up, and about noon all the boats came together for the last time. I had no mast or sail in mine, but I made a mast out of a spare oar and hoisted a boat-awning for a sail, with a boat-hook for a yard. She was certainly over-masted, but I had the satisfaction of knowing that with the wind aft I could beat the other two. I had to wait for them. Then we all had a look at the captain's chart, and, after a sociable meal of hard bread and water, got our last instructions. These were simple: steer north, and keep together as much as possible. "Be careful with that jury-rig, Marlow," said the captain; and Mahon, as I sailed proudly past his boat, wrinkled his curved nose and hailed, "You will sail that ship of yours under water, if you don't look out, young fellow." He was a malicious old man – and may the deep sea where he sleeps now rock him gently, rock him tenderly to the end of time!

'Before sunset a thick rain-squall passed over the two boats, which were far astern, and that was the last I saw of them for a time. Next day I sat steering my cockle-shell – my first command – with nothing but water and sky around me. I did sight in the afternoon the upper sails of a ship far away, but said nothing, and my men did not notice her. You see I was afraid she might be homeward bound, and I had no mind to turn back from the portals of the East. I was steering for Java – another blessed name – like Bankok, you know. I steered many days.

'I need not tell you what it is to be knocking about in an open boat. I remember nights and days of calm, when we pulled, we pulled, and the boat seemed to stand still, as if bewitched within the circle of the sea horizon. I remember the heat, the deluge of rain-squalls that kept us baling for dear life (but filled our water-cask), and I remember sixteen hours on end with a mouth dry as a cinder and a steering-oar over the stern to keep my first command head on to a breaking sea. I did not know how good a man I was till then. I remember the drawn faces, the dejected figures of my two men, and I remember my youth

34

and the feeling that will never come back any more – the feeling that I could last for ever, outlast the sea, the earth, and all men; the deceitful feeling that lures us on to joys, to perils, to love, to vain effort – to death; the triumphant conviction of strength, the heat of life in the handful of dust, the glow in the heart that with every year grows dim, grows cold, grows small, and expires – and expires, too soon, too soon – before life itself.

'And this is how I see the East. I have seen its secret places and have looked into its very soul; but now I see it always from a small boat, a high outline of mountains, blue and afar in the morning; like faint mist at noon; a jagged wall of purple at sunset. I have the feel of the oar in my hand, the vision of a scorching blue sea in my eyes. And I see a bay, a wide bay, smooth as glass and polished like ice, shimmering in the dark. A red light burns far off upon the gloom of the land, and the night is soft and warm. We drag at the oars with aching arms, and suddenly a puff of wind, a puff faint and tepid and laden with strange odours of blossoms, of aromatic wood, comes out of the still night – the first sigh of the East on my face. That I can never forget. It was impalpable and enslaving, like a charm, like a whispered promise of mysterious delight.

'We had been pulling this finishing spell for eleven hours. Two pulled, and he whose turn it was to rest sat at the tiller. We had made out the red light in that bay and steered for it, guessing it must mark some small coasting port. We passed two vessels, outlandish and high-sterned, sleeping at anchor, and, approaching the light, now very dim, ran the boat's nose against the end of a jutting wharf. We were blind with fatigue. My men dropped the oars and fell off the thwarts as if dead. I made fast to a pile. A current rippled softly. The scented obscurity of the shore was grouped into vast masses, a density of colossal clumps of vegetation, probably – mute and fantastic shapes. And at their foot the semicircle of a bench gleamed faintly, like an illusion. There was not a light, not a stir, not a sound. The mysterious East faced me, perfumed like a flower, silent like death, dark like a grave.

'And I sat weary beyond expression, exulting like a conqueror, sleepless and entranced as if before a profound, a fateful enigma.

'A splashing of oars, a measured dip reverberating on the

level of water, intensified by the silence of the shore into loud claps, made me jump up. A boat, a European boat, was coming in. I invoked the name of the dead; I hailed: *Judea* ahoy! A thin shout answered.

'It was the captain. I had beaten the flagship by three hours, and I was glad to hear the old man's voice again, tremulous and tired. "Is it you, Marlow?" "Mind the end of that jetty, sir," I cried.

'He approached cautiously, and brought up with the deep-sea lead-line which he had saved – for the underwriters. I eased my painter and fell alongside. He sat, a broken figure at the stern, wet with dew, his hands clasped in his lap. His men were asleep already. "I had a terrible time of it," he murmured. "Mahon is behind – not very far." We conversed in whispers, in low whispers, as if afraid to wake up the land. Guns, thunder, earthquakes would not have awakened the men just then.

'Looking round as we talked, I saw away at sea a bright light travelling in the night. "There's a steamer passing the bay," I said. She was not passing, she was entering, and she even came close and anchored. "I wish," said the old man, "you would find out whether she is English. Perhaps they could give us a passage somewhere." He seemed nervously anxious. So by dint of punching and kicking I started one of my men into a state of somnambulism, and giving him an oar, took another and pulled towards the lights of the steamer.

'There was a murmur of voices in her, metallic hollow clangs of the engine-room, footsteps on the deck. Her ports shone, round like dilated eyes. Shapes moved about, and there was a shadowy man high up on the bridge. He heard my oars.

'And then, before I could open my lips, the East spoke to me, but it was in a Western voice. A torrent of words was poured into the enigmatical, the fateful silence; outlandish, angry words, mixed with words and even whole sentences of good English, less strange but even more surprising. The voice swore and cursed violently; it riddled the solemn peace of the bay by a volley of abuse. It began by calling me Pig, and from that went crescendo into unmentionable adjectives – in English. The man up there raged aloud in two languages, and with a sincerity in his fury that almost convinced me I had, in some way, sinned against the harmony of the universe. I could hardly see him, but began to think he would work himself into a fit.

'Suddenly he ceased, and I could hear him snorting and blowing like a porpoise. I said –

' "What steamer is this, pray?"

' "Eh? What's this? And who are you?"

' "Castaway crew of an English barque burnt at sea. We came here tonight. I am the second mate. The captain is in the long-boat, and wishes to know if you would give us a passage somewhere."

' "Oh, my goodness! I say ... This is the *Celestial* from Singapore on her return trip. I'll arrange with your captain in the morning, ... and, ... I say, ... did you hear me just now?"

' "I should think the whole bay heard you."

' "I thought you were a shore-boat. Now, look here – this infernal lazy scoundrel of a caretaker has gone to sleep again – curse him. The light is out, and I nearly ran foul of the end of this damned jetty. This is the third time he plays me this trick. Now, I ask you, can anybody stand this kind of thing? It's enough to drive a man out of his mind. I'll report him ... I'll get the Assistant Resident to give him the sack, by ... ! See – there's no light. It's out, isn't it? I take you to witness the light's out. There should be a light, you know. A red light on the –"

' "There was a light," I said, mildly.

' "But it's out, man! What's the use of talking like this? You can see for yourself it's out – don't you? If you had to take a valuable steamer along this Godforsaken coast you would want a light, too. I'll kick him from end to end of his miserable wharf. You'll see if I don't. I will –"

' "So I may tell my captain you'll take us?" I broke in.

' "Yes, I'll take you. Good night," he said, brusquely.

'I pulled back, made fast again to the jetty, and then went to sleep at last. I had faced the silence of the East. I had heard some of its language. But when I opened my eyes again the silence was as complete as though it had never been broken. I was lying in a flood of light, and the sky had never looked so far, so high, before. I opened my eyes and lay without moving.

'And then I saw the men of the East – they were looking at me. The whole length of the jetty was full of people. I saw brown, bronze, yellow faces, the black eyes, the glitter, the colour of an Eastern crowd. And all these beings stared without a murmur, without a sigh, without a movement. They stared down at the boats, at the sleeping men who at night had come to them from the sea. Nothing moved. The fronds of palms stood still against the sky. Not a branch stirred along the shore, and the brown roofs of hidden houses peeped through the green foliage, through the big leaves that hung shining and still like leaves forged of heavy metal. This was the East of the ancient navigators, so old, so mysterious, resplendent and sombre, living and unchanged, full of danger and promise. And these were the men. I sat up suddenly. A wave of movement passed through the crowd from end to end, passed along the heads, swayed the bodies, ran along the jetty like a ripple on the water, like a breath of wind on a field – and all was still again. I see it now – the wide sweep of the bay, the glittering sands, the wealth of green infinite and varied, the sea blue like the sea of a dream, the crowd of attentive faces, the blaze of vivid colour – the water reflecting it all, the curve of the shore, the jetty, the high-sterned outlandish craft floating still, and the three boats with the tired men from the West sleeping, unconscious of the land and the people and of the violence of sunshine. They slept thrown across the thwarts, curled on bottom-boards, in the careless attitudes of death. The head of the old skipper, leaning back in the stern of the long-boat, had fallen on his breast, and he looked as though he would never wake. Farther out old Mahon's face was upturned to the sky, with the long white beard spread out on his breast, as though he had been shot where he sat at the tiller; and a man, all in a heap in the bows of the boat, slept with both arms embracing the stem-head and with his cheek laid on the gunwale. The East looked at them without a sound.

'I have known its fascination since; I have seen the mysterious shores, the still water, the lands of brown nations, where a stealthy Nemesis lies in wait, pursues, overtakes so many of the conquering race, who are proud of their wisdom, of their know-ledge, of their strength. But for me all the East is contained in that vision of my youth. It is all in that moment when I opened my young eyes on it. I came upon it from a tussle with the sea – and I was young – and I saw it looking at me. And this is all that is left of it! Only a moment; a moment of strength, of romance, of glamour – of youth! ... A flick of sunshine upon a strange shore, the time to remember, the time for a sigh, and – good-bye! – Night – Good-bye ... !'

He drank.

'Ah! The good old time – the good old time. Youth and the sea. Glamour and the sea! The good, strong sea, the salt, bitter sea, that could whisper to you and roar at you and knock your breath out of you.'

He drank again.

'By all that's wonderful it is the sea, I believe, the sea itself – or is it youth alone? Who can tell? But you here – you all had something out of life: money, love – whatever one gets on shore – and, tell me, wasn't that the best time, that time when we were young at sea; young and had nothing, on the sea that gives nothing, except hard knocks – and sometimes a chance to feel your strength – that only – what you all regret?'

And we all nodded at him: the man of finance, the man of accounts, the man of law, we all nodded at him over the polished table that like a still sheet of brown water reflected our faces, lined, wrinkled; our faces marked by toil, by deceptions, by success, by love; our weary eyes looking still, looking always, looking anxiously for something out of life, that while it is expected is already gone – has passed unseen, in a sigh, in a flash – together with the youth, with the strength, with the romance of illusions.

THE END OF THE TETHER

I

For a long time after the course of the steamer *Sofala* had been altered for the land, the low swampy coast had retained its appearance of a mere smudge of darkness beyond a belt of glitter. The sunrays fell violently upon the calm sea – seemed to shatter themselves upon an adamantine surface into sparkling dust, into a dazzling vapour of light that blinded the eye and wearied the brain with its unsteady brightness.

Captain Whalley did not look at it. When his Serang, approaching the roomy cane arm-chair which he filled capably, had informed him in a low voice that the course was to be altered, he had risen at once and had remained on his feet, face forward, while the head of his ship swung through a quarter of a circle. He had not uttered a single word, not even the word to steady the helm. It was the Serang, an elderly, alert, little Malay, with a very dark skin, who murmured the order to the helmsman. And then slowly Captain Whalley sat down again in the arm-chair on the bridge and fixed his eyes on the deck between his feet.

He could not hope to see anything new upon this lane of the sea. He had been on these coasts for the last three years. From Low Cape to Malantan the distance was fifty miles, six hours' steaming for the old ship with the tide, or seven against. Then you steered straight for the land, and by-and-by three palms would appear on the sky, tall and slim, and with their dishevelled heads in a bunch, as if in confidential criticism of the dark mangroves. The *Sofala* would be headed towards the sombre strip of the coast, which at a given moment, as the ship closed with it obliquely, would show several clean shining fractures – the brimful estuary of a river. Then on through a brown liquid, three parts water and one part black earth, on and on between the low shores, three parts black earth, and one part brackish water, the *Sofala* would plough her way upstream, as she had done once every month for these seven years or more, long before he was aware of her existence, long before he had ever thought of having anything to do with her and her invariable voyages. The old ship ought to have known the road better than her men, who had not been kept so long at it without a change; better than the faithful Serang, whom he had brought over from his last ship to keep the captain's watch; better than he himself, who had been her captain for the last three years only. She could always be depended upon to make her courses. Her compasses were never out. She was no trouble at all to take about, as if her great age had given her knowledge, wisdom, and steadiness. She made her landfalls to a degree of the bearing, and almost to a minute of her allowed time. At any moment, as he sat on the bridge without looking up, or lay sleepless in his bed, simply by reckoning the days and the hours he could tell where he was – the precise spot of the beat. He knew it well, too, this monotonous huckster's round, up and down the Straits; he knew its order and its sights and its people. Malacca to begin with, in at daylight and out at dusk, to cross over with a rigid phosphorescent wake this highway of the Far East. Darkness and gleams on the water, clear stars on a black sky, perhaps the lights of a home steamer keeping her unswerving course in the middle, or maybe the elusive shadow of a native craft with her mat sails flitting by silently – and low land on the other side in sight at daylight. At noon the three palms of the next place of call, up a sluggish river. The only white man residing there was a retired young sailor, with whom he had become friendly in the course of many voyages. Sixty miles farther on there was another place of call, a deep bay with only a couple of houses on the beach. And so on, in and out, picking up coastwise cargo here and there, and finishing with a hundred miles' steady steaming through the maze of an archipelago of small islands up to a large native town at the end of the beat. There was a three days' rest for the old ship before he started her again in inverse order, seeing the same shores from another bearing, hearing the same voices in the same places, back again to the *Sofala*'s port of registry on the great highway to the East, where he would take up a berth nearly opposite the big stone pile of the harbour office till it was time to start again on the old round of 1,600 miles and thirty days. Not a very enterprising life, this, for Captain Whalley, Henry Whalley, otherwise Daredevil Harry Whalley, of the *Condor*, a famous clipper in her day. No. Not a very enterprising life for a man who had served famous firms, who had sailed famous ships (more than one or two of them his own); who had made famous passages, had been the pioneer of new routes and new trades; who had steered across the unsurveyed tracts of the South Seas, and had seen the sun rise on uncharted islands. Fifty years at sea, and forty out in the East ('a pretty thorough apprenticeship,' he used to remark smilingly), had made him honourably known to a generation of shipowners and merchants in all the ports from Bombay clear over to where the East merges into the West upon the coast of the two Americas. His fame remained writ, not very large but plain enough, on the Admiralty charts. Was there not some- where between Australia and China a Whalley Island and a Condor Reef? On that dangerous coral formation the celebrated clipper had hung stranded for three days, her captain and crew throwing her cargo overboard with one hand and with the other, as it were, keeping off her a flotilla of savage war-canoes. At that time neither the island nor the reef had any official existence. Later the officers of her Majesty's steam-vessel *Fusilier*, des- patched to make a survey of the route, recognized in the adop- tion of these two names the enterprise of the man and the solidity of the ship. Besides, as any one who cares may see, the *General Directory* vol. ii, p. 410, begins the description of the 'Malotuor Whalley Passage' with the words: 'This advantageous route, first discovered in 1850 by Captain Whalley in the ship *Condor*,' etc., and ends by recommending it warmly to sailing vessels leaving the China ports for the south in the months from December to April inclusive.

This was the clearest gain he had out of life. Nothing could rob him of this kind of fame. The piercing of the Isthmus of Suez, like the breaking of a dam, had let in upon the East a flood of new ships, new men, new methods of trade. It had changed the face of the Eastern seas and the very spirit of their life; so that his early experiences meant nothing whatever to the new generation of seamen.

In those bygone days he had handled many thousands of pounds of his employers' money and of his own; he had attended faithfully, as by law a shipmaster is expected to do, to the con- flicting interests of owners, charterers, and underwriters. He had never lost a ship or consented to a shady transaction; and he had lasted well, outlasting in the end the conditions that had gone to the making of his name. He had buried his wife (in the Gulf of Petchili), had married off his daughter to the man of her unlucky choice, and had lost more than an ample competence in the crash of the notorious Travancore and Deccan Banking Corporation, whose downfall had shaken the East like an earthquake. And he was sixty-seven years old.

2

HIS age sat lightly enough on him; and of his ruin he was not ashamed. He had not been alone to believe in the stability of the Banking Corporation. Men whose judgement in matters of finance was as expert as his seamanship had commended the prudence of his investments, and had themselves lost much money in the great failure. The only difference between him and them was that he had lost his all. And yet not his all. There had remained to him from his lost fortune a very pretty little barque, *Fair Maid*, which he had bought to occupy his leisure of a retired sailor – 'to play with,' as he expressed it himself.

He had formally declared himself tired of the sea the year preceding his daughter's marriage. But after the young couple had gone to settle in Melbourne he found out that he could not make himself happy on shore. He was too much of a merchant sea-captain for mere yachting to satisfy him. He wanted the illusion of affairs; and his acquisition of the *Fair Maid* preserved the continuity of his life. He introduced her to his acquaintances in various ports as 'my last command'. When he grew too old to be trusted with a ship, he would lay her up and go ashore to be buried, leaving directions in his will to have the barque towed out and scuttled decently in deep water on the day of the funeral. His daughter would not grudge him the satisfaction of knowing that no stranger would handle his last command after him. With the fortune he was able to leave her, the value of a 500-ton barque was neither here nor there. All this would be said with a jocular twinkle in his eye: the vigorous old man had too much vitality for the sentimentalism of regret; and a little wistfully withal, because he was at home in life, taking a genuine pleasure in its feelings and its possessions; in the dignity of his reputation and his wealth, in his love for his daughter, and in his satisfaction with the ship – the plaything of his lonely leisure.

He had the cabin arranged in accordance with his simple ideal of comfort at sea. A big bookcase (he was a great reader) occupied one side of his stateroom; the portrait of his late wife, a flat bituminous oil-painting representing the profile and one long black ringlet of a young woman, faced his bedplace. Three chronometers ticked him to sleep and greeted him on waking with the tiny competition of their beats. He rose at five every day. The officer of the morning watch, drinking his early cup of coffee aft by the wheel, would hear through the wide orifice of the copper ventilators all the splashings, blowings, and splutterings of his captain's toilet. These noises would be followed by a sustained deep murmur of the Lord's Prayer recited in a loud earnest voice. Five minutes afterwards the head and shoulders of Captain Whalley emerged out of the companion-hatchway. Invariably he paused for a while on the stairs, looking all round at the horizon; upwards at the trim of the sails; inhaling deep draughts of the fresh air. Only then he would step out on the poop, acknowledging the hand raised to the peak of the cap with a majestic and benign 'Good morning to you'. He walked the deck till eight scrupulously. Sometimes, not above twice a year, he had to use a thick cudgel-like stick on account of a stiffness in the hip – a slight touch of rheumatism, he supposed. Otherwise he knew nothing of the ills of the flesh. At the ringing of the breakfast bell he went below to feed his canaries, wind up the chronometers, and take the head of the table. From there he had before his eyes the big carbon photographs of his daughter, her husband, and two fat-legged babies – his grandchildren – set in black frames into the maple-wood bulkheads of the cuddy. After breakfast he dusted the glass over these portraits himself with a cloth, and brushed the oil painting of his wife with a plummet kept suspended from a small brass hook by the side of the heavy gold frame. Then with the door of his state-room shut, he would sit down on the couch under the portrait to read a chapter out of a thick pocket Bible – her Bible. But on some days he only sat

47

there for half an hour with his finger between the leaves and the closed book resting on his knees. Perhaps he had remembered suddenly how fond of boat-sailing she used to be.

She had been a real shipmate and a true woman, too. It was like an article of faith with him that there never had been, and never could be, a brighter, cheerier home anywhere afloat or ashore than his home under the poop-deck of the *Condor*, with the big main cabin all white and gold, garlanded as if for a perpetual festival with an unfading wreath. She had decorated the centre of every panel with a cluster of home flowers. It took her a twelvemonth to go round the cuddy with this labour of love. To him it had remained a marvel of painting, the highest achievement of taste and skill; and as to old Swinburne, his mate, every time he came down to his meals he stood transfixed with admiration before the progress of the work. You could almost smell these roses, he declared, sniffing the faint flavour of turpentine which at that time pervaded the saloon, and (as he confessed afterwards) made him somewhat less hearty than usual in tackling his food. But there was nothing of the sort to interfere with his enjoyment of her singing. 'Mrs Whalley is a regular out-and-out nightingale, sir,' he would pronounce with a judicial air after listening profoundly over the skylight to the very end of the piece. In fine weather, in the second dog-watch, the two men could hear her trills and roulades going on to the accompaniment of the piano in the cabin. On the very day they got engaged he had written to London for the instrument; but they had been married for over a year before it reached them, coming out round the Cape. The big case made part of the first direct general cargo landed in Hongkong harbour – an event that to the men who walked the busy quays of today seemed as hazily remote as the dark ages of history. But Captain Whalley could in a half-hour of solitude live again all his life, with its romance, its idyl, and its sorrow. He had to close her eyes himself. She went away from under the ensign like a sailor's wife, a sailor herself at heart. He had read the service over her, out of her own prayer-book, without a break in his voice. When he raised his eyes he could see old Swinburne facing him with his cap pressed to his breast, and his rugged, weather-beaten, impassive face streaming with drops of water like a lump of chipped red granite in a shower. It was all very well for that old sea-dog to cry. He had to read on to the end; but after the splash he did not remember much of what happened for the next few days. An elderly sailor of the crew, deft at needlework, put together a mourning frock for the child out of one of her black skirts.

He was not likely to forget; but you cannot dam up life like a sluggish stream. It will break out and flow over a man's troubles, it will close upon a sorrow like the sea upon a dead body, no matter how much love has gone to the bottom. And the world is not bad. People had been very kind to him; especially Mrs Gardner, the wife of the senior partner in Gardner, Patteson & Co., the owners of the *Condor*. It was she who volunteered to look after the little one, and in due course took her to England (something of a journey in those days, even by the overland mail route) with her own girls to finish her education. It was ten years before he saw her again.

As a little child she had never been frightened of bad weather; she would beg to be taken up on deck in the bosom of his oilskin coat to watch the big seas hurling themselves upon the *Condor*. The swirl and crash of the waves seemed to fill her small soul with a breathless delight. 'A good boy spoiled,' he used to say of her in joke. He had named her Ivy because of the sound of the word, and obscurely fascinated by a vague association of ideas. She had twined herself tightly round his heart, and he intended her to cling close to her father as to a tower of strength; forgetting while she was little, that in the nature of things she would probably elect to cling to someone else. But he loved life well enough for even that event to give him a certain satisfaction, apart from his more intimate feeling of loss.

After he had purchased the *Fair Maid* to occupy his loneliness, he hastened to accept a rather unprofitable freight to Australia simply for the opportunity of seeing his daughter in her own home. What made him dissatisfied there was not to see that she clung now to somebody else, but that the prop she had selected seemed on closer examination 'a rather poor stick' – even in the matter of health. He disliked his son-in-law's studied civility perhaps more than his method of handling the sum of money he had given Ivy at her marriage. But of his apprehensions, he said nothing. Only on the day of his departure, with the hall-door open all ready, holding her hands and looking steadily into her eyes, he had said, 'You know, my dear, all I have is for you and the chicks. Mind you write to me openly.' She had answered him by an almost imperceptible movement of her head. She resembled her mother in the colour of her eyes, and in character – and also in this, that she understood him without many words.

Sure enough she had to write; and some of these letters made Captain Whalley lift his white eye-brows. For the rest he considered he was reaping the true reward for his life by being thus able to produce on demand whatever was needed. He had not enjoyed himself so much in a way since his wife had died. Characteristically enough his son-in-law's punctuality in failure caused him at a distance to feel a sort of kindness towards the man. The fellow was so perpetually being jammed on a lee shore that to charge it all to his reckless navigation would be manifestly unfair. No, no! He knew well what that meant. It was bad luck. His own had been simply marvellous, but he had seen in his life too many good men – seamen and others – go under with the sheer weight of bad luck not to recognize the fatal signs. For all that, he was cogitating on the best way of tying up very strictly every penny he had to leave, when with a preliminary rumble of rumours (whose first sound reached him in Shanghai as it happened), the shock of the big failure came; and, after passing through the phases of stupor, of incredulity, of indignation, he had to accept the fact that he had nothing to speak of to leave.

Upon that, as if he had only waited for this catastrophe, the unlucky man, away there in Melbourne, gave up his unprofitable game, and sat down – in an invalid's bath-chair at that, too. 'He will never walk again,' wrote the wife. For the first time in his life Captain Whalley was a bit staggered.

The *Fair Maid* had to go to work in bitter earnest now. It was no longer a matter of preserving alive the memory of Daredevil Harry Whalley in the Eastern Seas, or of keeping an old man in pocket-money and clothes, with, perhaps, a bill for a few hundred first-class cigars thrown in at the end of the year. He would have to buckle-to, and keep her going hard on a scant allowance of gilt for the ginger-bread scrolls at her stem and stern.

This necessity opened his eyes to the fundamental changes of the world. Of his past only the familiar names remained, here and there, but the things and the men, as he had known them, were gone. The name of Gardner, Patteson & Co. was still displayed on the walls of warehouses by the waterside, on the brass plates and window-panes in the business quarters of more than one Eastern port, but there was no longer a Gardner or a Patteson in the firm. There was no longer for Captain Whalley an arm-chair and a welcome in the private office, with a bit of business ready to be put in the way of an old friend, for the sake of bygone services. The husbands of the Gardner girls sat behind the desks in that room where, long after he had left the employ, he had kept his right of entrance in the old man's time. Their ships now had yellow funnels with black tops, and a time-table of appointed routes like a confounded service of tramways. The winds of December and June were all one to them; their captains (excellent young men he doubted not) were, to be sure, familiar with Whalley Island, because of late years the Government had established a white fixed light on the north end (with a red danger sector over the Condor Reef), but most of them would have been extremely surprised to hear that a flesh-and-blood Whalley still existed – an old man going about the world trying to pick up a cargo here and there for his little barque.

And everywhere it was the same. Departed the men who would have nodded appreciatively at the mention of his name, and would have thought themselves bound in honour to do something for Dare-devil Harry Whalley. Departed the opportunities which he would have known how to seize; and gone with them the white-winged flock of clippers that lived in the boisterous uncertain life of the winds, skimming big fortunes out of the foam of the seas. In a world that pared down the profits to an irreducible minimum, in a world that was able to count its disengaged tonnage twice over every day and in which lean charters were snapped up by cable three months in advance, there were no chances of fortune for an individual wandering haphazard with a little barque – hardly indeed any room to exist.

He found it more difficult from year to year. He suffered greatly from the smallness of remittances he was able to send his daughter. Meantime he had given up good cigars, and even in the matter of inferior cheroots limited himself to six a day. He never told her of his difficulties, and she never enlarged upon her struggle to live. Their confidence in each other needed no explanations, and their perfect understanding endured without protestations of gratitude or regret. He would have been shocked if she had taken it into her head to thank him in so many words, but he found it perfectly natural that she should tell him she needed two hundred pounds.

He had come in with the *Fair Maid* in ballast to look for a freight in the *Sofala*'s port of registry, and her letter met him there. Its tenor was that it was no use mincing matters. Her only resource was in opening a boarding-house, for which the prospects, she judged, were good. Good enough, at any rate, to make her tell him frankly that with two hundred pounds she could make a start. He had torn the envelope open, hastily, on deck, where it was handed to him by the ship-chandler's runner, who had brought his mail at the moment of anchoring. For the second time in his life he was appalled, and remained stock-still at the cabin door with the paper trembling between his fingers. Open a boarding-house! Two hundred pounds for a start! The only resource! And he did not know where to lay his hands on two hundred pence.

All that night Captain Whalley walked the poop of his anchored ship, as though he had been about to close with the land in thick weather, and uncertain of his position after a run of many grey days without a sight of sun, moon, or stars. The black night twinkled with the guiding lights of seamen and the steady straight lines of lights on shore; and all around the *Fair Maid* the riding lights of ships cast trembling trails upon the water of the roadstead. Captain Whalley saw not a gleam anywhere till the dawn broke and he found out that his clothing was soaked through with the heavy dew.

His ship was awake. He stopped short, stroked his wet beard, and descended the poop ladder backwards, with tired feet. At the sight of him the chief officer, lounging about sleepily on the quarterdeck, remained open-mouthed in the middle of a great early-morning yawn.

'Good morning to you,' pronounced Captain Whalley,

solemnly, passing into the cabin. But he checked himself in the doorway, and without looking back, 'By the bye,' he said, 'there should be an empty wooden case put away in the lazarette. It has not been broken up – has it?'

The mate shut his mouth, and then asked as if dazed, 'What empty case, sir?'

'A big flat packing-case belonging to that painting in my room. Let it be taken up on deck and tell the carpenter to look it over. I may want to use it before long.'

The chief officer did not stir a limb till he had heard the door of the captain's stateroom slam within the cuddy. Then he beckoned aft the second mate with his forefinger to tell him that there was something 'in the wind'.

When the bell rang Captain Whalley's authoritative voice boomed out through a closed door, 'Sit down and don't wait for me.' And his impressed officers took their places, exchanging looks and whispers across the table. What! No breakfast? And after apparently knocking about all night on deck, too! Clearly, there was something in the wind. In the skylight above their heads, bowed earnestly over the plates, three wire cages rocked and rattled to the restless jumping of the hungry canaries; and they could detect the sounds of their 'old man's' deliberate movements within his stateroom. Captain Whalley was methodically winding up the chronometers, dusting the portrait of his late wife, getting a clean white shirt out of the drawers, making himself ready in his punctilious, unhurried manner to go ashore. He could not have swallowed a single mouthful of food that morning. He had made up his mind to sell the *Fair Maid*.

3

JUST at that time the Japanese were casting far and wide for ships of European build, and he had no difficulty in finding a purchaser, a speculator who drove a hard bargain, but paid cash down for the *Fair Maid*, with a view to a profitable resale. Thus it came about that Captain Whalley found himself on a certain afternoon descending the steps of one of the most important post-offices of the East with a slip of bluish paper in his hand. This was the receipt of a registered letter enclosing a draft for two hundred pounds, and addressed to Melbourne. Captain Whalley pushed the paper into his waistcoat-pocket, took his stick from under his arm, and walked down the street.

It was a recently opened and untidy thoroughfare with rudimentary side-walks and a soft layer of dust cushioning the whole width of the road. One end touched the slummy street of Chinese shops near the harbour, the other drove straight on, without houses, for a couple of miles, through patches of jungle-like vegetation, to the yard gates of the new Consolidated Docks Company. The crude frontages of the new Government buildings alternated with the blank fencing of vacant plots, and the view of the sky seemed to give an added spaciousness to the broad vista. It was empty and shunned by natives after business hours, as though they had expected to see one of the tigers from the neighbourhood of the New Waterworks on the hill coming at a loping canter down the middle to get a Chinese shopkeeper for supper. Captain Whalley was not dwarfed by the solitude of the grandly planned street. He had too fine a presence for that. He was only a lonely figure walking purposefully, with a great white beard like a pilgrim, and with a thick stick that resembled a weapon. On one side the new Courts of Justice had a low and unadorned portico of squat columns half concealed by a few old trees left in the approach. On the other the pavilion wings of the new Colonial Treasury came out to the line of the street. But Captain Whalley, who had now no ship and no home, remembered in passing that on that very site when he first came out from England there had stood a fishing village, a few mat huts erected on piles between a muddy tidal creek and a miry pathway that went writhing into a tangled wilderness without any docks or waterworks.

No ship – no home. And his poor Ivy away there had no home either. A boarding-house is no sort of home though it may get you a living. His feelings were horribly rasped by the idea of the boarding-house. In his rank of life he had that truly aristocratic temperament characterized by a scorn of vulgar gentility and by prejudiced views as to the derogatory nature of certain occupations. For his own part he had always preferred sailing merchant ships (which is a straightforward occupation) to buying and selling merchandise of which the essence is to get the better of somebody in a bargain – an undignified trial of wits at best. His father had been Colonel Whalley (retired) of the H.E.I. Company's service, with very slender means besides his pension, but with distinguished connections. He could remember as a boy how frequently waiters at the inns, country tradesmen and small people of that sort, used to 'My Lord' the old warrior on the strength of his appearance.

Captain Whalley himself (he would have entered the Navy if his father had not died before he was fourteen) had something of a grand air which would have suited an old and glorious admiral; but he became lost like a straw in the eddy of a brook amongst the swarm of brown and yellow humanity filling a thoroughfare, that by contrast with the vast and empty avenue he had left seemed as narrow as a lane and absolutely riotous with life. The walls of the houses were blue; the shops of the Chinamen yawned like cavernous lairs; heaps of nondescript merchandise overflowed the gloom of the long range of arcades, and the fiery serenity of sunset took the middle of the street from end to end with a glow like the reflection of a fire. It fell on the bright colours and the dark faces of the bare-footed crowd, on the pallid yellow backs of the half-naked jostling coolies, on the accoutrements of a tall Sikh trooper with a parted beard and fierce moustaches on sentry before the gate of the police compound. Looming very big above the heads in a red haze of dust, the tightly packed car of the cable tramway navigated cautiously up the human stream, with the incessant blare of its horn, in the manner of a steamer groping in a fog.

Captain Whalley emerged like a diver on the other side, and in the desert shade between the walls of closed warehouses removed his hat to cool his brow. A certain disrepute attached to the calling of a landlady of a boarding-house. These women were said to be rapacious, unscrupulous, untruthful; and though he condemned no class of his fellow-creatures – God forbid ! – these were suspicions to which it was unseemly that a Whalley should lay herself open. He had not expostulated with her, however. He was confident she shared his feelings; he was sorry for her; he trusted her judgement; he considered it a merciful dispensation that he could help her once more – but in his aristo-cratic heart of hearts he would have found it more easy to recon-cile himself to the idea of her turning seamstress. Vaguely he remembered reading years ago a touching piece called the 'Song of the Shirt'. It was all very well making songs about poor women. The granddaughter of Colonel Whalley, the landlady of a boarding-house! Pooh! He replaced his hat, dived into two pockets, and stopping a moment to apply a flaring match to the end of a cheap cheroot, blew an embittered cloud of smoke at a world that could hold such surprises.

Of one thing he was certain – that she was the own child of a clever mother. Now he had got over the wrench of parting with his ship, he perceived clearly that such a step had been unavoid-able. Perhaps he had been growing aware of it all along with an unconfessed knowledge. But she, far away there, must have had an intuitive perception of it, with the pluck to face that truth and the courage to speak out – all the qualities which had made her mother a woman of such excellent counsel.

It would have had to come to that in the end! It was fortunate she had forced his hand. In another year or two it would have been an utterly barren sale. To keep the ship going he had been involving himself deeper every year. He was defenceless before the insidious work of adversity, to whose more open assaults he could present a firm front; like a cliff that stands unmoved the open battering of the sea, with a lofty ignorance of the treach-erous backwash undermining its base. As it was, every liability satisfied, her request answered, and owing no man a penny, there remained to him from the proceeds a sum of five hundred pounds to put away safely. In addition he had upon his person some forty odd dollars – enough to pay his hotel bill, providing he did not linger too long in the modest bedroom where he had taken refuge.

Scantily furnished, and with a waxed floor, it opened into one of the side-verandahs. The straggling building of bricks, as airy as a bird-cage, resounded with the incessant flapping of rat-tan screens worried by the wind between the whitewashed square pillars of the seafront. The rooms were lofty, a ripple of sunshine flowed over the ceilings; and the periodical invasions of tourists from some passenger steamer in the harbour flitted through the wind-swept dusk of the apartments with the tumult of their unfamiliar voices and impermanent presences, like relays of migratory shades condemned to speed headlong round the earth without leaving a trace. The babble of their irruptions ebbed out as suddenly as it had arisen; the draughty corridors and the long chairs of the verandahs knew their sight-seeing hurry or their prostrate repose no more; and Captain Whalley, substantial and dignified, left well nigh alone in the vast hotel by each light-hearted skurry, felt more and more like a stranded tourist with no aim in view, like a forlorn traveller without a home. In the solitude of his room he smoked thoughtfully, gazing at the two sea-chests which held all that he could call his own in this world. A thick roll of charts in a sheath of sailcloth leaned in a corner; the flat packing-case containing the portrait in oils and the three carbon photographs had been pushed under the bed. He was tired of discussing terms, of assisting at surveys, of all the routine of the business. What to the other parties was merely the sale of a ship was to him a momentous event involving a radically new view of existence. He knew that after this ship there would be no other; and the hopes of his youth, the exercise of his abilities, every feeling and achievement of his manhood, had been indissolubly connected with ships. He had served ships; he had owned ships; and even the years of his actual retirement from the sea had been made bearable by the idea that he had only to stretch out his hand full of money to get a ship. He had been at liberty to feel as though he were the owner of all the ships in the world. The selling of this one was weary work; but when she passed from him at last, when he signed the last receipt, it was as though all the ships had gone out of the world together, leaving him on the shore of inaccessible oceans with seven hundred pounds in his hands.

Striding firmly, without haste, along the quay, Captain Whalley averted his glances from the familiar roadstead. Two generations of seamen born since his first day at sea stood between him and all these ships at the anchorage. His own was sold, and he had been asking himself, What next?

From the feeling of loneliness, of inward emptiness – and of loss, too, as if his very soul had been taken out of him forcibly – there had sprung at first a desire to start right off and join his daughter. 'Here are the last pence,' he would say to her; 'take them, my dear. And here's your old father: you must take him, too.'

His soul recoiled, as if afraid of what lay hidden at the bottom of this impulse. Give up! Never! When one is thoroughly weary all sorts of nonsense come into one's head. A pretty gift it would have been for a poor woman – this seven hundred pounds with the incumbrance of a hale old fellow more than likely to last for years and years to come. Was he not as fit to die in harness as any of the youngsters in charge of these anchored ships out yonder? He was as solid now as ever he had been. But as to who would give him work to do, that was another matter. Were he, with his appearance and antecedents, to go about looking for a junior's berth, people, he was afraid, would not take him seriously; or else if he succeeded in impressing them, he would maybe obtain their pity, which would be like stripping yourself naked to be kicked. He was not anxious to give himself away for less than nothing. He had no use for anybody's pity. On the other hand, a command – the only thing he could try for with due regard for common decency – was not likely to be lying in wait for him at the corner of the next street. Commands don't go a-begging now-adays. Ever since he had come ashore to carry out the business of the sale he had kept his ears open, but had heard no hint of one being vacant in the port. And even if there had been one, his successful past itself stood in his way. He had been his own employer too long. The only credential he could produce was the testimony of his whole life. What better recommendation could any one require? But vaguely he felt that the unique document would be looked upon as an archaic curiosity of the Eastern waters, a screed traced in obsolete words – in a half-forgotten language.

4

REVOLVING these thoughts, he strolled on near the railings of the quay, broad-chested, without a stoop, as though his big shoulders had never felt the burden of the loads that must be carried between the cradle and the grave. No single betraying fold or line of care disfigured the reposeful modelling of his face. It was full and untanned; and the upper part emerged, massively quiet, out of the downward flow of silvery hair, with the striking delicacy of its clear complexion and the powerful width of the forehead. The first cast of his glance fell on you candid and swift, like a boy's; but because of the ragged snowy thatch of the eyebrows the affability of his attention acquired the character of a keen and searching scrutiny. With age he had put on flesh a little, had increased his girth like an old tree presenting no symptoms of decay; and even the opulent, lustrous ripple of white hairs upon his chest seemed an attribute of unquenchable vitality and vigour.

Once rather proud of his great bodily strength, and even of his personal appearance, conscious of his worth, and firm in his rectitude, there had remained to him, like the heritage of departed prosperity, the tranquil bearing of a man who had proved himself fit in every sort of way for the life of his choice. He strode on squarely under the projecting brim of an ancient Panama hat. It had a low crown, a crease through its whole diameter, a narrow black ribbon. Imperishable and a little discoloured, this headgear made it easy to pick him out from afar on thronged wharves and in the busy streets. He had never adopted the comparatively modern fashion of pipeclayed cork helmets. He disliked the form; and he hoped he could manage to keep a cool head to the end of his life without all these contrivances for hygienic ventilation. His hair was cropped close, his linen always of immaculate whiteness; a suit of thin grey flannel, worn threadbare but scrupulously brushed, floated about his burly limbs, adding to his bulk by the looseness of its cut. The years had mellowed the good-humoured, imperturbable audacity of his prime into a temper carelessly serene; and the leisurely tapping of his iron-shod stick accompanied his footfalls with a self-confident sound on the flagstones. It was impossible to connect such a fine presence and this unruffled aspect with the belittling troubles of poverty; the man's whole existence appeared to pass before you, facile and large, in the freedom of means as ample as the clothing of his body.

The irrational dread of having to break into his five hundred pounds for personal expenses in the hotel disturbed the steady poise of his mind. There was no time to lose. The bill was running up. He nourished the hope that this five hundred would perhaps be the means, if everything else failed, of obtaining some work which, keeping his body and soul together (not a matter of great outlay), would enable him to be of use to his daughter. To his mind it was her own money which he employed, as it were, in backing her father and solely for her benefit. Once at work, he would help her with the greater part of his earnings; he was good for many years yet, and this boarding-house business, he argued to himself, whatever the prospects, could not be much of a gold-mine from the first start. But what work? He was ready to lay hold of anything in an honest way so that it came quickly to his hand; because the five hundred pounds must be preserved intact for eventual use. That was the great point. With the entire five hundred one felt a substance at one's back; but it seemed to him that should he let it dwindle to four-fifty or even four-eighty, all the efficiency would be gone out of the money, as though there were some magic power in the round figure. But what sort of work?

Confronted by that haunting question as by an uneasy ghost, for whom he had no exorcizing formula, Captain Whalley stopped short on the apex of a small bridge spanning steeply the bed of a canalized creek with granite shores. Moored between the square blocks a sea-going Malay prau floated half hidden under the arch of masonry, with her spars lowered down, without a sound of life on board, and covered from stem to stern with a ridge of palm-leaf mats. He had left behind him the overheated pavements bordered by the stone frontages that, like the sheer face of cliffs, followed the sweep of the quays; and an unconfined spaciousness of orderly and sylvan aspect opened before him its wide plots of rolled grass, like pieces of green carpet smoothly pegged out, its long ranges of trees lined up in colossal porticos of dark shafts roofed with a vault of branches.

Some of these avenues ended at the sea. It was a terraced shore; and beyond, upon the level expanse, profound and glistening like the gaze of a dark-blue eye, an oblique band of stippled purple lengthened itself indefinitely through the gap between a couple of verdant twin islets. The masts and spars of a few ships far away, hull down in the outer roads, sprang straight from the water in a fine maze of rosy lines pencilled on the clear shadow of the eastern board. Captain Whalley gave them a long glance. The ship, once his own, was anchored out there. It was staggering to think that it was open to him no longer to take a boat at the jetty and get himself pulled off to her when the evening came. To no ship. Perhaps never more. Before the sale was concluded, and till the purchase-money had been paid, he had spent daily some time on board the *Fair Maid*. The money had been paid this very morning, and now, all at once, there was positively no ship that he could go on board of when he liked; no ship that would need his presence in order to do her work – to live. It seemed an incredible state of affairs, something too bizarre to last. And the sea was full of craft of all sorts. There was that prau lying so still swathed in her shroud of sewn palm-leaves – she, too, had her indispensable man. They lived through each other, this Malay he had never seen, and this high-sterned thing of no size that seemed to be resting after a long journey. And of all the ships in sight, near and far, each was provided with a man, the man without whom the finest ship is a dead thing, a floating and purposeless log.

After his one glance at the roadstead he went on since there was nothing to turn back for, and the time must be got through somehow. The avenues of big trees ran straight over the Esplanade, cutting each other at diverse angles, columnar below and luxuriant above. The interlaced boughs high up there seemed to slumber; not a leaf stirred overhead: and the reedy cast-iron lamp-posts in the middle of the road, gilt like sceptres diminished in a long perspective, with their globes of white porcelain atop, resembling a barbarous decoration of ostriches' eggs displayed in a row. The flaming sky kindled a tiny crimson spark upon the glistening surface of each glassy shell.

With his chin sunk a little, his hands behind his back, and the end of his stick marking the gravel with a faint wavering line at his heels, Captain Whalley reflected that if a ship without a man was like a body without a soul, a sailor without a ship was of not much more account in this world than an aimless log adrift upon the sea. The log might be sound enough by itself, tough of fibre, and hard to destroy – but what of that! And a sudden sense of irremediable idleness weighted his feet like a great fatigue.

A succession of open carriages came bowling along the newly opened sea-road. You could see across the wide grass-plots the discs of vibration made by the spokes. The bright domes of the parasols swayed lightly outwards like full-blown blossoms on the rim of a vase; and the quiet sheet of dark-blue water, crossed by a bar of purple, made a background for the spinning wheels and the high action of the horses, whilst the turbaned heads of the Indian servants elevated above the line of the sea horizon glided rapidly on the paler blue of the sky. In an open space near the little bridge each turn-out trotted smartly in a wide curve away from the sunset; then pulling up sharp, entered the main alley in a long slow-moving file with the great red stillness of the sky at the back. The trunks of mighty trees stood all touched with red on the same side, the air seemed aflame under the high foliage, the very ground under the hoofs of the horses was red. The wheels turned solemnly; one after another the sunshades drooped, folding their colours like gorgeous flowers shutting their petals at the end of the day. In the whole half-mile of human beings no voice uttered a distinct word, only a faint thudding noise went on mingled with slight jingling sounds, and the motionless heads and shoulders of men and women sitting in couples emerged stolidly above the lowered hoods – as if wooden. But one carriage and pair coming late did not join the line.

It fled along in a noiseless roll; but on entering the avenue one of the dark bays snorted, arching his neck and shying against the steel-tipped pole; a flake of foam fell from the bit upon the point of a satiny shoulder, and the dusky face of the coachman leaned forward at once over the hands taking a fresh grip of the reins. It was a long dark-green landau, having a dignified and buoyant motion between the sharply curved C-springs, and a sort of strictly official majesty in its supreme elegance. It seemed more roomy than is usual, its horses seemed slightly bigger, the appointments a shade more perfect, the servants perched somewhat higher on the box. The dresses of three women – two young and pretty, and one, handsome, large, of mature age – seemed to fill completely the shallow body of the carriage. The fourth face was that of a man, heavy lidded, distinguished and sallow, with a sombre, thick, iron-grey imperial and moustaches, which somehow had the air of solid appendages. His Excellency –

The rapid motion of that one equipage made all the others appear utterly inferior, blighted, and reduced to crawl painfully at a snail's pace. The landau distanced the whole file in a sort of sustained rush; the features of the occupants whirling out of sight left behind an impression of fixed stares and impassive vacancy; and after it had vanished in full flight as it were, notwithstanding the long line of vehicles hugging the curb at a walk, the whole lofty vista of the avenue seemed to lie open and emptied of life in the enlarged impression of an august solitude.

Captain Whalley had lifted his head to look, and his mind, disturbed in its meditation, turned with wonder (as men's minds will do) to matters of no importance. It struck him that it was to this port, where he had just sold his last ship, that he had come with the very first he had ever owned, and with his head full of a plan for opening a new trade with a distant part of the Archipelago. The then governor had given him no end of encouragement. No Excellency he – this Mr Denham – this governor with his jacket off; a man who tended night and day, so to speak, the growing prosperity of the settlement with the self-forgetful devotion of a nurse for a child she loves; a lone bachelor who lived as in a camp with the few servants and his three dogs in what was called then the Government Bungalow : a low-roofed structure on the half-cleared slope of a hill, with a new flagstaff in front and a police orderly on the verandah. He remembered toiling up that hill under a heavy sun for his audience; the unfurnished aspect of the cool shaded room; the long table covered at one end with piles of papers, and with two guns, a brass telescope, a small bottle of oil with a feather stuck in the neck at the other – and the flattering attention given to him by the man in power. It was an undertaking full of risk he had come to expound, but a twenty minutes' talk in the Government Bungalow on the hill had made it go smoothly from the start. And as he was retiring Mr Denham, already seated before the papers, called out after him, 'Next month the *Dido* starts for a cruise that way, and I shall request her captain officially to give you a look in and see how you get on.' The *Dido* was one of the smart frigates on the China station – and five-and-thirty years make a big slice of time. Five-and-thirty years ago an enterprise like his had for the colony enough importance to be looked after by a Queen's ship. A big slice of time. Individuals were of some account then. Men like himself; men, too, like poor Evans, for instance, with his red face, his coal-black whiskers, and his restless eyes, who had set up the first patent slip for repairing small ships, on the edge of the forest, in a lonely bay three miles up the coast. Mr Denham had encouraged that enterprise, too, and yet somehow poor Evans had ended by dying at home deucedly hard up. His son, they said, was squeezing oil out of cocoa-nuts for a living on some God-forsaken islet of the Indian Ocean; but it was from that patent slip in a lonely wooded bay that had sprung the work-shops of the Consolidated Docks Company, with its three graving basins carved out of solid rock, its wharves, its jetties, its electric-light plant, its steam-power houses – with its gigantic sheer-legs, fit to lift the heaviest weight ever carried afloat, and whose head could be seen like the top of a queer white monument peeping over bushy points of land and sandy promontories, as you approached the New Harbour from the west.

There had been a time when men counted: there were not so many carriages in the colony then, though Mr Denham, he fancies, had a buggy. And Captain Whalley seemed to be swept out of the great avenue by the swirl of a mental backwash. He remembered muddy shores, a harbour without quays, the one solitary wooden pier (but that was a public work) jutting out crookedly, the first coal-sheds erected on Monkey Point, that caught fire mysteriously and smouldered for days, so that amazed ships came into a roadstead full of sulphurous fog, and the sun hung blood-red at midday. He remembered the things, the faces, and something more besides – like the faint flavour of a cup quaffed to the bottom, like a subtle sparkle of the air that was not to be found in the atmosphere of today.

In this evocation, swift and full of detail like a flash of magnesium light into the niches of a dark memorial hall, Captain Whalley contemplated things once important, the efforts of small men, the growth of a great place, but now robbed of all consequence by the greatness of accomplished facts, by hopes greater still; and they gave him for a moment such an almost physical grip upon time, such a comprehension of our unchangeable feelings, that he stopped short, struck the ground with his stick, and ejaculated mentally, 'What the devil am I doing here!' He seemed lost in a sort of surprise; but he heard his name called out in wheezy tones once, twice – and turned on his heels slowly.

He beheld then, waddling towards him autocratically, a man of an old-fashioned and gouty aspect, with hair as white as his own, but with shaved, florid cheeks, wearing a necktie – almost a neckcloth – whose stiff ends projected far beyond his chin; with round legs, round arms, a round body, a round face – generally producing the effect of his short figure having been distended by means of an air-pump as much as the seams of his clothing would stand. This was the Master-Attendant of the port. A master-attendant is a superior sort of harbour-master; a person, out in the East, of some consequence in his sphere; a Government official, a magistrate for the waters of the port, and possessed of vast but ill-defined disciplinary authority over seamen of all classes. This particular Master-Attendant was reported to consider it miserably inadequate, on the ground that it did not include the power of life and death. This was a jocular exaggeration. Captain Eliott was fairly satisfied with his position, and nursed no inconsiderable sense of such power as he had. His conceited and tyrannical disposition did not allow him to let it dwindle in his hands for want of use. The uproarious, choleric frankness of his comments on people's character and conduct caused him to be feared at bottom. Though in conversation many pretended not to mind him in the least, others would only smile sourly at the mention of his name, and there were even some who dared to pronounce him 'a meddlesome old ruffian'. But for almost all of them one of Captain Eliott's outbreaks was nearly as distasteful to face as a chance of annihilation.

5

As soon as he had come up quite close he said, mouthing in a growl –

'What's this I hear, Whalley? Is it true you're selling the *Fair Maid*?'

Captain Whalley, looking away, said the thing was done – money had been paid that morning; and the other expressed at once his approbation of such an extremely sensible proceeding. He had got out of his trap to stretch his legs, he explained, on his way home to dinner. Sir Frederick looked well at the end of his time. Didn't he?

Captain Whalley could not say; had only noticed the carriage going past.

The Master-Attendant, plunging his hands into the pockets of an alpaca jacket inappropriately short and tight for a man of his age and appearance, strutted with a slight limp, and with his head reaching only to the shoulder of Captain Whalley, who walked easily, staring straight before him. They had been good comrades years ago, almost intimates. At the time when Whalley commanded the renowned *Condor*, Eliott had charge of the nearly as famous *Ringdove* for the same owners; and when the appointment of Master-Attendant was created, Whalley would have been the only other serious candidate. But Captain Whalley, then in the prime of life, was resolved to serve no one but his own auspicious Fortune. Far away, tending his hot irons, he was glad to hear the other had been successful. There was a worldly suppleness in bluff Ned Elliott that would serve him well in that sort of official appointment. And they were so dissimilar at bottom that as they came slowly to the end of the avenue before the Cathedral, it had never come into Whalley's head that he might have been in that man's place – provided for to the end of his days.

The sacred edifice, standing in solemn isolation amongst the converging avenues of enormous trees, as if to put grave thoughts of heaven into the hours of ease, presented a closed Gothic portal to the light and glory of the west. The glass of the rosace above the ogive glowed like fiery coal in the deep carvings of a wheel of stone. The two men faced about.

'I'll tell you what they ought to do next, Whalley,' growled Captain Eliott suddenly.

'Well?'

'They ought to send a real live lord out here when Sir Frederick's time is up. Eh?'

Captain Whalley perfunctorily did not see why a lord of the

right sort should not do as well as any one else. But this was not the other's point of view.

'No, no. Place runs itself. Nothing can stop it now. Good enough for a lord,' he growled in short sentences. 'Look at the changes in our own time. We need a lord here now. They have got a lord in Bombay.'

He dined once or twice every year at the Government House – a many-windowed, arcaded palace upon a hill laid out in roads and gardens. And lately he had been taking about a duke in his Master-Attendant's steam-launch to visit the harbour improvements. Before that he had 'most obligingly' gone out in person to pick out a good berth for the ducal yacht. Afterwards he had an invitation to lunch on board. The duchess herself lunched with them. A big woman with a red face. Complexion quite sunburnt. He should think ruined. Very gracious manners. They were going on to Japan . . .

He ejaculated these details for Captain Whalley's edification, pausing to blow out his cheeks as if with a pent-up sense of importance, and repeatedly protruding his thick lips till the blunt crimson end of his nose seemed to dip into the milk of his moustache. The place ran itself; it was fit for any lord; it gave no trouble except in its Marine department – in its Marine department, he repeated twice, and after a heavy snort began to relate how the other day her Majesty's Consul-General in French Cochin-China had cabled to him – in his official capacity – asking for a qualified man to be sent over to take charge of a Glasgow ship whose master had died in Saigon.

'I sent word of it to the officers' quarters in the Sailors' Home,' he continued, while the limp in his gait seemed to grow more accentuated with the increasing irritation of his voice. 'Place's full of them. Twice as many men as there are berths going in the local trade. All hungry for an easy job. Twice as many – and – What d'you think, Whalley? . . .'

He stopped short; his hands, clenched and thrust deeply downwards, seemed ready to burst the pockets of his jacket. A slight sigh escaped Captain Whalley.

'Hey? You would think they would be falling over each other. Not a bit of it. Frightened to go home. Nice and warm out here to lie about a verandah waiting for a job. I sit and wait in my office. Nobody. What did they suppose? That I was going to sit there like a dummy with the Consul-General's cable before me? Not likely. So I looked up a list of them I keep by me and sent word for Hamilton – the worst loafer of them all – and just made him go. Threatened to instruct the steward of the Sailors' Home to have him turned out neck and crop. He did not think the berth was good enough – if you – please. "I've your little record by me," said I. "You came ashore here eighteen months ago, and you haven't done six months' work since. You are in debt for your board now at the Home, and I suppose you reckon the Marine Office will pay in the end. Eh? So it shall; but if you don't take this chance, away you go to England, assisted passage, by the first homeward steamer that comes along. You are no better than a pauper. We don't want any white paupers here." I scared him. But look at the trouble all this gave me.'

'You would not have had any trouble,' Captain Whalley said almost involuntarily, 'if you had sent for me.'

Captain Eliott was immensely amused; he shook with laughter as he walked. But suddenly he stopped laughing. A vague recollection had crossed his mind. Hadn't he heard it said at the time of the Travancore and Deccan smash that poor Whalley had been cleaned out completely. 'Fellow's hard up, by heavens!' he thought; and at once he cast a sidelong upwards glance at his companion. But Captain Whalley was smiling austerely straight before him, with a carriage of the head inconceivable in a penniless man – and he became reassured. Impossible. Could not have lost everything. That ship had been only a hobby of his. And the reflection that a man who had confessed to receiving that very morning a presumably large sum of money was not likely to spring upon him a demand for a small loan put him entirely at his ease again. There had come a long pause in their talk, however, and not knowing how to begin again, he growled out soberly, 'We old fellows ought to take a rest now.'

'The best thing for some of us would be to die at the oar,' Captain Whalley said, negligently.

'Come, now. Aren't you a bit tired by this time of the whole show?' muttered the other, sullenly.

'Are you?'

Captain Eliott was. Infernally tired. He only hung on to his berth so long in order to get his pension on the highest scale before he went home. It would be no better than poverty, anyhow; still, it was the only thing between him and the workhouse. And he had a family. Three girls, as Whalley knew. He gave 'Harry, old boy,' to understand that these three girls were a source of the greatest anxiety and worry to him. Enough to drive a man distracted.

'Why? What have they been doing now?' asked Captain Whalley with a sort of amused absent-mindedness.

'Doing! Doing nothing. That's just it. Lawn-tennis and silly novels from morning to night . . .'

If one of them at least had been a boy! But all three! And, as ill-luck would have it, there did not seem to be any decent young fellows left in the world. When he looked around in the club he saw only a lot of conceited popinjays too selfish to think of making a good woman happy. Extreme indigence stared him in the face with all that crowd to keep at home. He had cherished the idea of building himself a little house in the country – in Surrey – to end his days in, but he was afraid it was out of the question . . . and his staring eyes rolled upwards with such a pathetic anxiety that Captain Whalley charitably nodded down at him, restraining a sort of sickening desire to laugh.

'You must know what it is yourself, Harry. Girls are the very devil for worry and anxiety.'

'Ay! But mine is doing well,' Captain Whalley pronounced slowly, staring to the end of the avenue.

The Master-Attendant was glad to hear this. Uncommonly glad. He remembered her well. A pretty girl she was.

Captain Whalley, stepping out carelessly, assented as if in a dream:

'She was pretty.'

The procession of carriages was breaking up.

One after another they left the file to go off at a trot, animating the vast avenue with their scattered life and movement; but soon the aspect of dignified solitude returned and took possession of the straight wide road. A syce in white stood at the head of a Burmah pony harnessed to a varnished two-wheel cart; and the whole thing waiting by the curb seemed no bigger than a child's toy forgotten under the soaring trees. Captain Eliott waddled up to it and made as if to clamber in, but refrained; and keeping one hand resting easily on the shaft, he changed the conversation from his pension, his daughters, and his poverty back again to the only other topic in the world – the Marine Office, the men and the ships of the port.

He proceeded to give instances of what was expected of him; and his thick voice drowsed in the still air like the obstinate droning of an enormous bumble-bee. Captain Whalley did not know what was the force or the weakness that prevented him from saying good night and walking away. It was as though he had been too tired to make the effort. How queer. More queer than any of Ned's instances. Or was it that overpowering sense of idleness alone that made him stand there and listen to these stories? Nothing very real had ever troubled Ned Eliott; and gradually he seemed to detect deep in, as if wrapped up in the gross wheezy rumble, something of the clear hearty voice of the young captain of the *Ringdove*. He wondered if he, too, had changed to the same extent; and it seemed to him that the voice of his old chum had not changed so very much – that the man was the same. Not a bad fellow the pleasant, jolly Ned Eliott, friendly, well up to his business – and always a bit of a humbug. He remembered how he used to amuse his poor wife. She could read him like an open book. When the *Condor* and the *Ringdove* happened to be in port together, she would frequently ask him to bring Captain Eliott to dinner. They had not met often since those old days. Not once in five years, perhaps. He regarded from under his white eyebrows this man he could not bring himself to take into his confidence at this juncture; and the other went on with his intimate outpourings, and as remote from his hearer as though he had been talking on a hill-top a mile away.

He was in a bit of a quandary now as to the steamer *Sofala*. Ultimately every hitch in the port came into his hands to undo. They would miss him when he was gone in another eighteen months, and most likely some retired naval officer had been pitchforked into the appointment – a man that would understand nothing and care less. That steamer was a coasting craft having a steady trade connection as far north as Tenasserim; but the trouble was she could get no captain to take her on her regular trip. Nobody would go in her. He really had no power, of course, to order a man to take a job. It was all very well to stretch a point on the demand of a consul-general, but . . .

'What's the matter with the ship?' Captain Whalley interrupted in measured tones.

'Nothing's the matter. Sound old steamer. Her owner has been in my office this afternoon tearing his hair.'

'Is he a white man?' asked Whalley in an interested voice.

'He calls himself a white man,' answered the Master-Attendant scornfully; 'but if so, it's just skin-deep and no more. I told him that to his face, too.'

'But who is he, then?'

'He's the chief engineer of her. See *that*, Harry?'

'I see,' Captain Whalley said, thoughtfully. 'The engineer. I see.'

How the fellow came to be a shipowner at the same time was quite a tale. He came out third in a home ship nearly fifteen years ago, Captain Eliott remembered, and got paid off after a bad sort of row both with his skipper and his chief. Anyway, they seemed jolly glad to get rid of him at all costs. Clearly a mutinous sort of chap. Well, he remained out here, a perfect nuisance, everlastingly shipped and unshipped, unable to keep a berth very long; pretty nigh went through every engine-room afloat belonging to the colony. Then suddenly, 'What do you think happened, Harry?'

Captain Whalley, who seemed lost in a mental effort as of doing a sum in his head, gave a slight start. He really couldn't imagine. The Master-Attendant's voice vibrated dully with hoarse emphasis. The man actually had the luck to win the second great prize in the Manila lottery. All these engineers and officers of ships took tickets in that gamble. It seemed to be a perfect mania with them all.

Everybody expected now that he would take himself off home with his money, and go to the devil in his own way. Not at all. The *Sofala*, judged too small and not quite modern enough for the sort of trade she was in, could be got for a moderate price from her owners, who had ordered a new steamer from Europe. He rushed in and bought her. This man had never given any signs of that sort of mental intoxication the mere fact of getting hold of a large sum of money may produce – not till he got a ship of his own; but then he went off his balance all at once: came bouncing into the Marine Office on some transfer business, with his hat hanging over his left eye and switching a little cane in his hand, and told each of the clerks separately that 'Nobody could put him out now. It was his turn. There was no one over him on earth, and there never would be either.' He swaggered and strutted between the desks, talking at the top of his voice, and trembling like a leaf all the while, so that the current business of the office was suspended for the time he was in there, and everybody in the big room stood open-mouthed looking at his antics. Afterwards he could be seen during the hottest hours of the day with his face as red as fire rushing along up and down the quays to look at his ship from different points of view: he seemed inclined to stop every stranger he came across just to let them know 'that there would be no longer any one over him; he had bought a ship; nobody on earth could put him out of his engine-room now'.

Good bargain as she was, the price of the *Sofala* took up pretty near all the lottery-money. He had left himself no capital to work with. That did not matter so much, for these were the halcyon days of steam coasting trade, before some of the home shipping firms had thought of establishing local fleets to feed their main lines. These, when once organized, took the biggest slices out of that cake, of course; and by-and-by a squad of confounded German tramps turned up east of Suez Canal and swept up all the crumbs. They prowled on the cheap to and fro along the coast and between the islands, like a lot of sharks in the water ready to snap up anything you let drop. And then the high old times were over for good; for years the *Sofala* had made no more, he judged, than a fair living. Captain Eliott looked upon it as his duty in every way to assist an English ship to hold her own; and it stood to reason that if for want of a captain the *Sofala* began to miss her trips she would very soon lose her trade. There was the quandary. The man was too impracticable. 'Too much of a beggar on horseback from the first,' he explained. 'Seemed to grow worse as the time went on. In the last three years he's run through eleven skippers; he had tried every single man here, outside of the regular lines. I had warned him before that this would not do. And now, of course, no one will look at the *Sofala*. I had one or two men up at my office and talked to them; but, as they said to me, what was the good of taking the berth to lead a regular dog's life for a month and then get the sack at the end of the first trip? The fellow, of course, told me it was all nonsense; there has been a plot hatching for years against him. And now it had come. All the horrid sailors in the port had conspired to bring him to his knees, because he was an engineer.' Captain Eliott emitted a throaty chuckle.

'And the fact is, that if he misses a couple more trips he need never trouble himself to start again. He won't find any cargo in his old trade. There's too much competition nowadays for people to keep their stuff lying about for a ship that does not turn up when she's expected. It's a bad lookout for him. He swears he will shut himself on board and starve to death in his cabin rather than sell her – even if he could find a buyer. And that's not likely in the least. Not even the Japs would give her insured value for her. It isn't like selling sailing-ships. Steamers *do* get out of date, besides getting old.'

'He must have laid by a good bit of money though,' observed Captain Whalley, quietly.

The Harbour-master puffed out his purple cheeks to an amazing size.

'Not a stiver, Harry. Not – a – single sti-ver.'

He waited; but as Captain Whalley, stroking his beard slowly, looked down on the ground without a word, he tapped him on the forearm, tiptoed, and said in a hoarse whisper –

'The Manila lottery has been eating him up.'

He frowned a little, nodding in tiny affirmative jerks. They all were going in for it; a third of the wages paid to ships' officers ('in my port,' he snorted) went to Manila. It was a mania. That fellow Massy had been bitten by it like the rest of them from the first; but after winning once he seemed to have persuaded himself he had only to try again to get another big prize. He had taken dozens and scores of tickets for every drawing since. What with this vice and his ignorance of affairs, ever since he had improvidently bought that steamer he had been more or less short of money.

This, in Captain Eliott's opinion, gave an opening for a

sensible sailor-man with a few pounds to step in and save that fool from the consequences of his folly. It was his craze to quarrel with his captains. He had had some really good men, too, who would have been too glad to stay if he would only let them. But no. He seemed to think he was no owner unless he was kicking somebody out in the morning and having a row with the new man in the evening. What was wanted for him was a master with a couple of hundred or so to take an interest in the ship on proper conditions. You don't discharge a man for no fault, only because of the fun of telling him to pack up his traps and go ashore, when you know that in that case you are bound to buy back his share. On the other hand, a fellow with an interest in the ship is not likely to throw up his job in a huff about a trifle. He had told Massy that. He had said: ' "This won't do, Mr Massy. We are getting very sick of you here in the Marine Office. What you must do now is to try whether you could get a sailor to join you as partner. That seems to be the only way." And that was sound advice, Harry.'

Captain Whalley, leaning on his stick, was perfectly still all over, and his hand, arrested in the act of stroking, grasped his whole beard. And what did the fellow say to that?

The fellow had the audacity to fly out at the Master-Attendant. He had received the advice in a most impudent manner. 'I didn't come here to be laughed at,' he had shrieked. 'I appeal to you as an Englishman and a shipowner brought to the verge of ruin by an illegal conspiracy of your beggarly sailors, and all you condescend to do for me is to tell me to go and get a partner !' ... The fellow had presumed to stamp with rage on the floor of the private office. Where was he going to get a partner? Was he being taken for a fool? Not a single one of that contemptible lot ashore at the 'Home' had twopence in his pocket to bless himself with. The very native curs in the bazaar knew that much ... 'And it's true enough, Harry,' rumbled Captain Eliott, judicially. 'They are much more likely one and all to owe money to the Chinamen in Denham Road for the clothes on their backs. "Well," said I, "you make too much noise over it for my taste, Mr Massy. Good morning." He banged the door after him; he dared to bang my door, confound his cheek !'

The head of the Marine department was out of breath with

indignation; then recollecting himself as it were, 'I'll end by being late to dinner – yarning with you here . . . wife doesn't like it.'

He clambered ponderously into the trap; leaned out sideways, and only then wondered wheezily what on earth Captain Whalley could have been doing with himself of late. They had had no sight of each other for years and years till the other day when he had seen him unexpectedly in the office.

What on earth . . .

Captain Whalley seemed to be smiling to himself in his white beard.

'The earth is big,' he said, vaguely.

The other, as if to test the statement, stared all round from his driving-seat. The Esplanade was very quiet; only from afar, from very far, a long way from the sea-shore, across the stretches of grass, through the long ranges of trees, came faintly the toot – toot – toot of the cable car beginning to roll before the empty peristyle of the Public Library on its three-mile journey to the New Harbour Docks.

'Doesn't seem to be so much room on it,' growled the Master-Attendant, 'since these Germans came along shouldering us at every turn. It was not so in our time.'

He fell into deep thought, breathing stertorously, as though he had been taking a nap open-eyed. Perhaps he, too, on his side, had detected in the silent pilgrim-like figure, standing there by the wheel, like an arrested wayfarer, the buried lineaments of the features belonging to the young captain of the *Condor*. Good fellow – Harry Whalley – never very talkative. You never knew what he was up to – a bit too off-hand with people of consequence, and apt to take a wrong view of a fellow's actions. Fact was he had a too good opinion of himself. He would have liked to tell him to get in and drive him home to dinner. But one never knew. Wife would not like it.

'And it's funny to think, Harry,' he went on in a big subdued drone, 'that of all the people on it there seems only you and I left to remember this part of the world as it used to be . . .'

He was ready to indulge in the sweetness of a sentimental mood had it not struck him suddenly that Captain Whalley, unstirring and without a word, seemed to be awaiting something –

perhaps expecting ... He gathered the reins at once and burst out in bluff hearty growls –

'Ha! My dear boy. The men we have known – the ships we've sailed – ay! and the things we've done ...'

The pony plunged – the syce skipped out of the way. Captain Whalley raised his arm.

'Good-bye.'

6

THE sun had set. And when, after drilling a deep hole with his stick, he moved from that spot the night had massed its army of shadows under the trees. They filled the eastern ends of the avenue as if only waiting the signal for a general advance upon the open spaces of the world; they were gathering low between the deep stone-faced banks of the canal. The Malay prau, half concealed under the arch of the bridge, had not altered its position a quarter of an inch. For a long time Captain Whalley stared down over the parapet, till at last the floating immobility of that beshrouded thing seemed to grow upon him into something inexplicable and alarming. The twilight abandoned the zenith; its reflected gleams left the world below, and the water of the canal seemed to turn into pitch. Captain Whalley crossed it.

The turning to the right, which was his way to his hotel, was only a very few steps farther. He stopped again (all the houses of the sea-front were shut up, the quayside was deserted, but for one or two figures of natives walking in the distance) and began to reckon the amount of his bill. So many days in the hotel at so many dollars a day. To count the days he used his fingers: plunging one hand into his pocket, he jingled a few silver coins. All right for three days more; and then, unless something turned up, he must break into the five hundred – Ivy's money – invested in her father. It seemed to him that the first meal coming out of that reserve would choke him – for certain. Reason was of no use. It was a matter of feeling. His feelings had never played him false.

He did not turn to the right. He walked on, as if there still had been a ship in the roadstead to which he could get himself pulled off in the evening. Far away, beyond the houses, on the slope of an indigo promontory closing the view of the quays, the slim column of a factory-chimney smoked quietly straight up into the clear air. A Chinaman, curled down in the stern of one of the half-dozen sampans floating off the end of the jetty, caught sight of a beckoning hand. He jumped up, rolled his pigtail round his head swiftly, tucked in two rapid movements his wide dark trousers high up his yellow thighs, and by a single, noiseless, finlike stir of the oars, sheered the sampan alongside the steps with the ease and precision of a swimming fish.

'Sofala,' articulated Captain Whalley from above; and the Chinaman, a new emigrant probably, stared upwards with a tense attention as if waiting to see the queer word fall visibly from the white man's lips. 'Sofala,' Captain Whalley repeated; and suddenly his heart failed him. He paused. The shores, the islets, the high ground, the low points, were dark: the horizon had grown sombre; and across the eastern sweep of the shore the white obelisk, marking the landing-place of the telegraph-cable, stood like a pale ghost on the beach before the dark spread of un-even roofs, intermingled with palms, of the native town. Captain Whalley began again:

'Sofala. Savee So-fa-la, John?'

This time the Chinaman made out that bizarre sound, and grunted his assent uncouthly, low down in his bare throat. With the first yellow twinkle of a star that appeared like the head of a pin stabbed deep into the smooth, pale, shimmering fabric of the sky, the edge of a keen chill seemed to cleave through the warm air of the earth. At the moment of stepping into the sampan to go and try for the command of the *Sofala* Captain Whalley shivered a little.

When on his return he landed on the quay again, Venus, like a choice jewel set low on the hem of the sky, cast a faint gold trail behind him upon the roadstead, as level as a floor made of one dark and polished stone. The lofty vaults of the avenues were black – all black overhead – and the porcelain globes on the lamp-posts resembled egg-shaped pearls, gigantic and luminous, displayed in a row whose farther end seemed to sink in the dis-tance, down to the level of his knees. He put his hands behind his back. He would now consider calmly the discretion of it before saying the final word tomorrow. His feet scrunched the gravel loudly – the discretion of it. It would have been easier to appraise had there been a workable alternative. The honesty of it was indubitable: he meant well by the fellow; and periodically his shadow leaped up intense by his side on the trunks of the trees, to lengthen itself, oblique and dim, far over the grass – repeating his stride.

The discretion of it. Was there a choice? He seemed already to have lost something of himself; to have given up to a hungry spectre something of his truth and dignity in order to live. But his life was necessary. Let poverty do its worst in exacting its toll of humiliation. It was certain that Ned Eliott had rendered him, without knowing it, a service for which it would have been impossible to ask. He hoped Ned would not think there had been something underhand in his action. He supposed that now when he heard of it he would understand – or perhaps he would only think Whalley an eccentric old fool. What would have been the good of telling him – any more than of blurting the whole tale to that man Massy? Five hundred pounds ready to invest. Let him make the best of that. Let him wonder. You want a captain – I want a ship. That's enough. B-r-r-r-r. What a disagreeable impression that empty, dark, echoing steamer had made upon him . . .

A laid-up steamer was a dead thing and no mistake; a sailing-ship somehow seems always ready to spring into life with the breath of the incorruptible heaven; but a steamer, thought Captain Whalley, with her fires out, without the warm whiffs from below meeting you on her decks, without the hiss of steam, the clangs of iron in her breast – lies there as cold and still and pulseless as a corpse.

In the solitude of the avenue, all black above and lighted below, Captain Whalley, considering the discretion of his course, met, as it were incidentally, the thought of death. He pushed it aside with dislike and contempt. He almost laughed at it; and in the unquenchable vitality of his age only thought with a kind of exultation how little he needed to keep body and soul together. Not a bad investment for the poor woman this solid carcass of her father. And for the rest – in case of anything – the agreement should be clear: the whole five hundred to be paid back to her integrally within three months. Integrally. Every penny. He was not to lose any of her money whatever else had to go – a little dignity – some of his self-respect. He had never before allowed anybody to remain under any sort of false impression as to himself. Well, let that go – for her sake. After all, he had never *said* anything misleading – and Captain Whalley felt himself corrupt to the marrow of his bones. He laughed a little with the intimate scorn of his worldly prudence. Clearly, with a fellow of that sort, and in the peculiar relation they were to stand to each other, it would not have done to blurt out everything. He did not like the fellow. He did not like his spells of fawning loquacity and bursts of resentfulness. In the end – a poor devil. He would not have liked to stand in his shoes. Men were not evil, after all. He did not like his sleek hair, his queer way of standing at right angles, with his nose in the air, and glancing along his shoulder at you. No. On the whole, men were not bad – they were only silly or unhappy.

Captain Whalley had finished considering the discretion of that step – and there was the whole long night before him. In the full light his long beard would glisten like a silver breast-plate covering his heart; in the spaces between the lamps his burly figure passed less distinct, loomed very big, wandering, and mysterious. No; there was not much real harm in men: and all the time a shadow marched with him, slanting on his left hand – which in the East is a presage of evil.

*

'Can you make out the clump of palms yet, Serang?' asked Captain Whalley from his chair on the bridge of the *Sofala* approaching the bar of Batu Beru.

'No, Tuan. By-and-by see.' The old Malay, in a blue dungaree suit, planted on his bony dark feet under the bridge awning, put his hands behind his back and stared ahead out of the innumerable wrinkles at the corners of his eyes.

Captain Whalley sat still, without lifting his head to look for himself. Three years – thirty-six times. He had made these palms thirty-six times from the southward. They would come into view at the proper time. Thank God, the old ship made her courses and distances trip after trip, as correct as clockwork. At last he murmured again —

'In sight yet?'

'The sun makes a very great glare, Tuan.'

'Watch well, Serang.'

'Ya, Tuan.'

A white man had ascended the ladder from the deck noiselessly, and had listened quietly to this short colloquy. Then he stepped out on the bridge and began to walk from end to end, holding up the long cherrywood stem of a pipe. His black hair lay plastered in long lanky wisps across the bald summit of his head; he had a furrowed brow, a yellow complexion, and a thick shapeless nose. A scanty growth of whisker did not conceal the contour of his jaw. His aspect was of brooding care; and sucking at a curved black mouthpiece, he presented such a heavy overhanging profile that even the Serang could not help reflecting sometimes upon the extreme unloveliness of some white men.

Captain Whalley seemed to brace himself up in his chair, but gave no recognition whatever to his presence. The other puffed jets of smoke; then suddenly —

'I could never understand that new mania of yours of having this Malay here for your shadow, partner.'

Captain Whalley got up from the chair in all his imposing stature and walked across to the binnacle, holding such an unswerving course that the other had to back away hurriedly, and remained as if intimidated, with the pipe trembling in his hand. 'Walk over me now,' he muttered in a sort of astounded and discomfited whisper. Then slowly and distinctly he said —

'I — am — not — dirt.' And then added defiantly, 'As you seem to think.'

The Serang jerked out —

'See the palms now, Tuan.'

Captain Whalley strode forward to the rail; but his eyes, instead of going straight to the point, with the assured keen glance of a sailor, wandered irresolutely in space, as though he, the discoverer of new routes, had lost his way upon this narrow sea.

Another white man, the mate, came up on the bridge. He was

tall, young, lean, with a moustache like a trooper, and something malicious in the eye. He took up a position beside the engineer. Captain Whalley with his back to them, inquired –

'What's on the log?'

'Eighty-five,' answered the mate quickly, and nudged the engineer with his elbow.

Captain Whalley's muscular hands squeezed the iron rail with an extraordinary force; his eyes glared with an enormous effort; he knitted his eyebrows, the perspiration fell from under his hat – and in a faint voice he murmured, 'Steady her, Serang – when she is on the proper bearing.'

The silent Malay stepped back, waited a little, and lifted his arm warningly to the helmsman. The wheel revolved rapidly to meet the swing of the ship. Again the mate nudged the engineer. But Massy turned upon him.

'Mr Sterne,' he said, violently, 'let me tell you – as a shipowner – that you are no better than a confounded fool.'

7

STERNE went down smirking and apparently not at all disconcerted, but the engineer Massy remained on the bridge, moving about with uneasy self-assertion. Everybody on board was his inferior – everyone without exception. He paid their wages and found them in their food. They ate more of his bread and pocketed more of his money than they were worth; and they had no care in the world, while he alone had to meet all the difficulties of shipowning. When he contemplated his position in all its menacing entirety, it seemed to him that he had been for years the prey of a band of parasites; and for years he had scowled at everybody connected with the *Sofala* except, perhaps, at the Chinese firemen who served to get her along. Their use was manifest: they were an indispensable part of the machinery of which he was the master.

When he passed along his decks he shouldered those he came across brutally; but the Malay deck hands had learned to dodge out of his way. He had to bring himself to tolerate them because of the necessary manual labour of the ship which must be done. He had to struggle and plan and scheme to keep the *Sofala* afloat – and what did he get for it? Not even enough respect. They could not have given him enough of that if all their thoughts and all their actions had been directed to that end. The vanity of possession, the vainglory of power, had passed away by this time, and there remained only the material embarrassments, the fear of losing that position which had turned out not worth having, and an anxiety of thought which no abject subservience of men could repay.

He walked up and down. The bridge was his own after all. He had paid for it; and with the stem of the pipe in his hand he would stop short at times as if to listen with a profound and concentrated attention to the deadened beat of the engines (his own engines) and the slight grinding of the steering chains upon the continuous low wash of water alongside. But for these sounds the ship might have been lying as still as if moored to a bank, and as silent as if abandoned by every living soul; only the coast, the low coast of mud and mangroves with the three palms in a bunch at the back, grew slowly more distinct in its long straight line; without a single feature to arrest attention. The native passengers of the *Sofala* lay about on mats under the awnings; the smoke of her funnel seemed the only sign of her life and connected with her gliding motion in a mysterious manner.

Captain Whalley on his feet, with a pair of binoculars in his hand and the little Malay Serang at his elbow, like an old giant attended by a wizened pigmy, was taking her over the shallow water of the bar.

This submarine ridge of mud, scoured by the stream out of the soft bottom of the river and heaped up far out on the hard bottom of the sea, was difficult to get over. The alluvial coast having no distinguishing marks, the bearings of the crossing-place had to be taken from the shape of the mountains inland. The guidance of a form flattened and uneven at the top like a grinder tooth, and of another smooth, saddle-backed summit, had to be searched for within the great unclouded glare that seemed to shift and float like a dry fiery mist, filling the air, ascending from the water, shrouding the distances, scorching to the eye. In this veil of light the near edge of the shore alone stood out almost coal-black with an opaque and motionless solidity. Thirty miles away the serrated range of the interior stretched across the horizon, its outlines and shades of blue, faint and tremulous like a background painted on airy gossamer on the quivering fabric of an impalpable curtain let down to the plain of alluvial soil; and the openings of the estuary appeared, shining white, like bits of silver let into the square pieces snipped clean and sharp out of the body of the land bordered with mangroves.

On the forepart of the bridge the giant and the pigmy muttered to each other frequently in quiet tones. Behind them Massy stood sideways with an expression of disdain and suspense on his face. His globular eyes were perfectly motionless, and he seemed to have forgotten the long pipe he held in his hand.

On the fore-deck below the bridge, steeply roofed with the white slopes of the awnings, a young lascar seaman had clambered outside the rail. He adjusted quickly a broad band of sail canvas under his armpits, and throwing his chest against it, leaned out far over the water. The sleeve of his thin cotton shirt, cut off close to the shoulder, bared his brown arm of full rounded form and with a satiny skin like a woman's. He swung it rigidly with the rotary and menacing action of a slinger: the 14-lb. weight hurtled circling in the air, then suddenly flew ahead as far as the curve of the bow. The wet thin line swished like scratched silk running through the dark fingers of the man, and the plunge of the lead close to the ship's side made a vanishing silvery scar upon the golden glitter; then after an interval the voice of the young Malay uplifted and longdrawn declared the depth of the water in his own language.

'Tiga stengah,' he cried after each splash and pause, gathering the line busily for another cast. 'Tiga stengah,' which means three fathom and a half. For a mile or so from seaward there was a uniform depth of water right up to the bar. 'Half-three. Half-three. Half-three,' – and his modulated cry, returned leisurely and monotonous, like the repeated call of a bird, seemed to float away in sunshine and disappear in the spacious silence of the empty sea and of a lifeless shore lying open, north and south, east and west, without the stir of a single cloud-shadow or the whisper of any other voice.

The owner-engineer of the *Sofala* remained very still behind the two seamen of different race, creed, and colour; the European with the time-defying vigour of his old frame, the little Malay, old, too, but slight and shrunken like a withered brown leaf blown by a chance wind under the mighty shadow of the other. Very busy looking forward at the land, they had not a glance to spare; and Massy, glaring at them from behind, seemed to resent their attention to their duty like a personal slight upon himself.

This was unreasonable; but he had lived in his own world of unreasonable resentments for many years. At last, passing his moist palm over the rare lanky wisps of coarse hair on the top of his yellow head, he began to talk slowly.

'A leadsman, you want! I suppose that's your correct mail-boat style. Haven't you enough judgement to tell where you are by looking at the land? Why, before I had been a twelvemonth in the trade I was up to that trick – and I am only an engineer. I can point to you from here where the bar is, and I could tell you besides that you are likely as not to stick her in the mud in about five minutes from now; only you would call it interfering, I suppose. And there's that written agreement of ours, that says I mustn't interfere.'

His voice stopped. Captain Whalley, without relaxing the set severity of his features, moved his lips to ask in a quick mumble –

'How near, Serang?'

'Very near now, Tuan,' the Malay muttered, rapidly.

'Dead slow,' said the Captain aloud in a firm tone.

The Serang snatched at the handle of the telegraph. A gong clanged down below. Massy with a scornful snigger walked off and put his head down the engine-room skylight.

'You may expect some rare fooling with the engines, Jack,' he bellowed. The space into which he stared was deep and full of gloom; and the grey gleams of steel down there seemed cool after the intense glare of the sea around the ship. The air, however, came up clammy and hot on his face. A short hoot on which it would have been impossible to put any sort of interpretation

84

came from the bottom cavernously. This was the way in which the second engineer answered his chief.

He was a middle-aged man with an inattentive manner, and apparently wrapped up in such a taciturn concern for his engines that he seemed to have lost the use of speech. When addressed directly his only answer would be a grunt or a hoot, according to the distance. For all the years he had been in the *Sofala* he had never been known to exchange as much as a frank Good-morning with any of his shipmates. He did not seem aware that men came and went in the world; he did not seem to see them at all. Indeed he never recognized his shipmates on shore. At table (the four white men of the *Sofala* messed together) he sat looking into his plate dispassionately, but at the end of the meal would jump up and bolt down below as if a sudden thought had impelled him to rush and see whether somebody had not stolen the engines while he dined. In port at the end of the trip he went ashore regularly, but no one knew where he spent his evenings or in what manner. The local coasting fleet had preserved a wild and incoherent tale of his infatuation for the wife of a sergeant in an Irish infantry regiment. The regiment, however, had done its turn of garrison duty there ages before, and was gone somewhere to the other side of the earth, out of men's knowledge. Twice or perhaps three times in the course of the year he would take too much to drink. On these occasions he returned on board at an earlier hour than usual; ran across the deck balancing himself with his spread arms like a tight-rope walker; and locking the door of his cabin, he would converse and argue with himself the livelong night in an amazing variety of tones; storm, sneer and whine with an inexhaustible persistence. Massy in his berth next door, raising himself on his elbow, would discover that his second had remembered the name of every white man that had passed through the *Sofala* for years and years back. He remembered the names of men that had died, that had gone home, that had gone to America: he remembered in his cups the names of men whose connection with the ship had been so short that Massy had almost forgotten its circumstances and could barely recall their faces. The inebriated voice on the other side of the bulkhead commented upon them all with an extraordinary and ingenious venom of scandalous inventions. It seems they had all offended him in some way, and in return he had found them all out. He muttered darkly; he laughed sardonically; he crushed them one after another; but of his chief, Massy, he babbled with an envious and naïve admiration. Clever scoundrel! Don't meet the likes of him every day. Just look at him. Ha! Great! Ship of his own. Wouldn't catch *him* going wrong. No fear – the beast! And Massy, after listening with a gratified smile to these artless tributes to his greatness, would begin to shout, thumping at the bulkhead with both fists –

'Shut up, you lunatic! Won't you let me go to sleep, you fool!'

But a half smile of pride lingered on his lips; outside the solitary lascar told off for night duty in harbour, perhaps a youth fresh from a forest village, would stand motionless in the shadows of the deck listening to the endless drunken gabble. His heart would be thumping with breathless awe of white men: the arbitrary and obstinate men who pursue inflexibly their incomprehensible purposes – beings with weird intonations in the voice, moved by unaccountable feelings, actuated by inscrutable motives.

8

FOR a while after his second's answering hoot Massy hung over the engine-room gloomily. Captain Whalley who, by the power of five hundred pounds, had kept his command for three years, might have been suspected of never having seen that coast before. He seemed unable to put down his glasses, as though they had been glued under his contracted eyebrows. This settled frown gave to his face an air of invincible and just severity; but his raised elbow trembled slightly, and the perspiration poured from under his hat as if a second sun had suddenly blazed up at the zenith by the side of the ardent still globe already there, in whose blinding white heat the earth whirled and shone like a mote of dust.

From time to time, still holding up his glasses, he raised his other hand to wipe his streaming face. The drops rolled down his cheeks, fell like rain upon the white hairs of his beard, and brusquely, as if guided by an uncontrollable and anxious impulse, his arm reached out to the stand of the engine-room telegraph.

The gong clanged down below. The balanced vibration of the dead-slow speed ceased together with every sound and tremor in the ship, as if the great stillness that reigned upon the coast had stolen in through her sides of iron and taken possession of her innermost recesses. The illusion of perfect immobility seemed to fall upon her from the luminous blue dome without a stain arching over a flat sea without a stir. The faint breeze she had made for herself expired, as if all at once the air had become too thick to budge; even the slight hiss of the water on her stem died out. The narrow, long hull, carrying its way without a ripple, seemed to approach the shoal water of the bar by stealth. The plunge of the lead with the mournful, mechanical cry of the lascar came at longer intervals; and the men on her bridge seemed to hold their breath. The Malay at the helm looked fixedly at the compass card, the Captain and the Serang stared at the coast.

Massy had left the skylight, and, walking flat-footed, had returned softly to the very spot on the bridge he had occupied before. A slow, lingering grin exposed his set of big white teeth : they gleamed evenly in the shade of the awning like the keyboard of a piano in a dusky room.

At last, pretending to talk to himself in excessive astonishment, he said not very loud —

'Stop the engines now. What next, I wonder?'

He waited, stooping from the shoulders, his head bowed, his glance oblique. Then raising his voice a shade —

'If I dared make an absurd remark I would say that you haven't the stomach to ...'

But a yelling spirit of excitement, like some frantic soul wandering unsuspected in the vast stillness of the coast, had seized upon the body of the lascar at the lead. The languid monotony of his sing-song changed to a swift, sharp clamour. The weight flew after a single whirr, the line whistled, splash followed splash in haste. The water had shoaled, and the man, instead of the drowsy tale of fathoms, was calling out the soundings in feet.

'Fifteen feet. Fifteen, fifteen ! Fourteen, fourteen ...'

Captain Whalley lowered the arm holding the glasses. It descended slowly as if by its own weight; no other part of his towering body stirred; and the swift cries with their eager warning note passed him by as though he had been deaf.

Massy, very still, and turning an attentive ear, had fastened his eyes upon the silvery, close-cropped back of the steady old head. The ship herself seemed to be arrested but for the gradual decrease of depth under her keel.

'Thirteen feet ... Thirteen! Twelve!' cried the leadsman anxiously below the bridge. And suddenly the barefooted Serang stepped away noiselessly to steal a glance over the side.

Narrow of shoulder, in a suit of faded blue cotton: an old grey felt hat rammed down on his head, with a hollow in the nape of his dark neck, and with his slender limbs, he appeared from the back no bigger than a boy of fourteen. There was a childlike impulsiveness in the curiosity with which he watched the spread of the voluminous, yellowish convolutions rolling up from below to the surface of the blue water like massive clouds driving slowly upwards on the unfathomable sky. He was not startled at the sight in the least. It was not doubt, but the certitude that the keel of the *Sofala* must be stirring the mud now, which made him peep over the side.

His peering eyes, set aslant in a face of the Chinese type, a little old face, immovable, as if carved in old brown oak, had informed him long before that the ship was not headed at the bar properly. Paid off from the *Fair Maid*, together with the rest of the crew, after the completion of the sale, he had hung, in his faded blue suit and floppy grey hat, about the doors of the Harbour Office, till one day, seeing Captain Whalley coming along to get a crew for the *Sofala*, he had put himself quietly in the way, with his bare feet in the dust and an upward mute glance. The eyes of his old commander had fallen on him favourably – it must have been an auspicious day – and in less than half an hour the white men in the 'Ofiss' had written his name on a document as Serang of the fire-ship *Sofala*. Since that time he had repeatedly looked at that estuary, upon that coast, from this bridge and from this side of the bar. The record of the visual world fell through his eyes upon his unsuspecting mind as on a sensitized plate through the lens of a camera. His knowledge was absolute and precise; nevertheless, had he been asked his opinion, and especially if questioned in the downright, alarming manner of white men, he would have displayed the hesitation of ignorance. He was certain of his facts — but such a certitude counted for little against the doubt what answer would be pleasing. Fifty years ago, in a jungle village, and before he was a day old, his father (who died without ever seeing a white face) had had his nativity cast by a man of skill and wisdom in astrology, because in the arrangement of the stars may be read the last word of human destiny. His destiny had been to thrive by the favour of various white men on the sea. He had swept the decks of ships, had tended their helms, had minded their stores, had risen at last to be a Serang; and his placid mind had remained as incapable of penetrating the simplest motives of those he served as they themselves were incapable of detecting through the crust of the earth the secret nature of its heart, which may be fire or may be stone. But he had no doubt whatever that the *Sofala* was out of the proper track for crossing the bar at Batu Beru.

It was a slight error. The ship could not have been more than twice her own length too far to the northward; and a white man at a loss for a cause (since it was impossible to suspect Captain Whalley of blundering ignorance, of want of skill, or of neglect) would have been inclined to doubt the testimony of his senses. It was some such feeling that kept Massy motionless, with his teeth laid bare by an anxious grin. Not so the Serang. He was not troubled by any intellectual mistrust of his senses. If his captain chose to stir the mud it was well. He had known in his life white men indulge in outbreaks equally strange. He was only genuinely interested to see what would come of it. At last, apparently satisfied, he stepped back from the rail.

He had made no sound: Captain Whalley, however, seemed to have observed the movements of his Serang. Holding his head rigidly, he asked with a mere stir of his lips —

'Going ahead still, Serang?'

'Still going a little, Tuan,' answered the Malay. Then added casually, 'She is over.'

The lead confirmed his words; the depth of water increased at every cast, and the soul of excitement departed suddenly from the lascar swung in the canvas belt over the *Sofala*'s side. Captain

Whalley ordered the lead in, set the engines ahead without haste, and averting his eyes from the coast directed the Serang to keep a course for the middle of the entrance.

Massy brought the palm of his hand with a loud smack against his thigh.

'You grazed on the bar. Just look astern and see if you didn't. Look at the track she left. You can see it plainly. Upon my soul, I thought you would! What made you do that? What on earth made you do that? I believe you are trying to scare me.'

He talked slowly, as it were circumspectly, keeping his promi-nent black eyes on his captain. There was also a slight plaintive note in his rising choler, for, primarily, it was the clear sense of a wrong suffered undeservedly that made him hate the man who, for a beggarly five hundred pounds, claimed a sixth part of the profits under the three years' agreement. Whenever his resent-ment got the better of the awe the person of Captain Whalley inspired he would positively whimper with fury.

'You don't know what to invent to plague my life out of me. I would not have thought that a man of your sort would con-descend . . .'

He paused, half hopefully, half timidly, whenever Captain Whalley made the slightest movement in the deck-chair, as though expecting to be conciliated by a soft speech or else rushed upon and hunted off the bridge.

'I am puzzled,' he went on again, with the watchful, unsmil-ing baring of his big teeth. 'I don't know what to think. I do believe you are trying to frighten me. You very nearly planted her on the bar for at least twelve hours, besides getting the engines choked with mud. Ships can't afford to lose twelve hours on a trip nowadays – as you ought to know very well, and do know very well to be sure, only . . .'

His slow volubility, the sideways cranings of his neck, the black glances out of the very corners of his eyes, left Captain Whalley unmoved. He looked at the deck with a severe frown. Massy waited for some little time, then began to threaten plain-tively.

'You think you've got me bound hand and foot in that agree-ment. You think you can torment me in any way you please. Ah! But remember it has another six weeks to run yet. There's time for me to dismiss you before the three years are out. You will do yet something that will give me the chance to dismiss you, and make you wait a twelvemonth for your money before you can take yourself off and pull out your five hundred, and leave me without a penny to get the new boilers for her. You gloat over the idea – don't you? I do believe you sit here gloating. It's as if I had sold my soul for five hundred pounds to be everlastingly damned in the end . . .'

He paused, without apparent exasperation, then continued evenly –

'. . . With the boilers worn out and the survey hanging over my head, Captain Whalley – Captain Whalley, I say, what do you do with your money? You must have stacks of money somewhere – a man like you must. It stands to reason. I am not a fool, you know, Captain Whalley – partner.'

Again he paused, as though he had done for good. He passed his tongue over his lips, gave a backward glance at the Serang conning the ship with quiet whispers and slight signs of the hand. The wash of the propeller sent a swift ripple, crested with dark froth, upon a long flat spit of black slime. The *Sofala* had entered the river; the trail she had stirred up over the bar was a mile astern of her now, out of sight, had disappeared utterly; and the smooth, empty sea along the coast was left behind in the glittering desolation of sunshine. On each side of her, low down, the growth of sombre twisted mangroves covered the semi-liquid banks; and Massy continued in his old tone, with an abrupt start, as if his speech had been ground out of him, like the tune of a music-box, by turning a handle.

'Though if anybody ever got the best of me, it is you. I don't mind saying this. I've said it – there! What more can you want? Isn't that enough for your pride, Captain Whalley? You got over me from the first. It's all of a piece, when I look back at it. You allowed me to insert that clause about intemperance without saying anything, only looking very sick when I made a point of it going in black and white. How could I tell what was wrong about you? There's generally something wrong somewhere. And, lo and behold! when you come on board it turns out that you've been in the habit of drinking nothing but water for years and years.'

His dogmatic, reproachful whine stopped. He brooded profoundly, after the manner of crafty and unintelligent men. It seemed inconceivable that Captain Whalley should not laugh at the expression of disgust that overspread the heavy, yellow countenance. But Captain Whalley never raised his eyes – sitting in his arm-chair, outraged, dignified, and motionless.

'Much good it was to me,' Massy remonstrated, monotonously, 'to insert a clause of dismissal for intemperance against a man who drinks nothing but water. And you looked so upset, too, when I read my draft in the lawyer's office that morning, Captain Whalley – you looked so crestfallen, that I made sure I had gone home on your weak spot. A shipowner can't be too careful as to the sort of skipper he gets. You must have been laughing at me in your sleeve all the blessed time ... Eh? What are you going to say?'

Captain Whalley had only shuffled his feet slightly. A dull animosity became apparent in Massy's sideways stare.

'But recollect that there are other grounds for dismissal. There's habitual carelessness, amounting to incompetence – there's gross and persistent neglect of duty. I am not quite as big a fool as you try to make me out to be. You have been careless of late – leaving everything to that Serang. Why! I've seen you letting that old fool of a Malay take bearings for you, as if you were too big to attend to your work yourself. And what do you call that silly touch-and-go manner in which you took the ship over the bar just now? You expect me to put up with that.'

Leaning on his elbow against the ladder abaft the bridge, Sterne, the mate, tried to hear, blinking the while from the distance at the second engineer, who had come up for a moment, and stood in the engine-room companion. Wiping his hands on a bunch of cotton waste, he looked about with indifference to the right and left at the river banks slipping astern of the *Sofala* steadily.

Massy turned full at the chair. The character of his whine became again threatening.

'Take care. I may yet dismiss you and freeze to your money for a year. I may ...'

But before the silent, rigid immobility of the man whose

money had come in the nick of time to save him from utter ruin, his voice died out in his throat.

'Not that I want you to go,' he resumed after a silence, and in an absurdly insinuating tone. 'I want nothing better than to be friends and renew the agreement, if you will consent to find another couple of hundred to help with the new boilers, Captain Whalley. I've told you before. She must have new boilers; you know it as well as I do. Have you thought this over?'

He waited, The slender stem of the pipe with its bulky lump of a bowl at the end hung down from his thick lips. It had gone out. Suddenly he took it from between his teeth and wrung his hands slightly.

'Don't you believe me?' He thrust the pipe bowl into the pocket of his shiny black jacket.

'It's like dealing with the devil,' he said. 'Why don't you speak? At first you were so high and mighty with me I hardly dared to creep about my own deck. Now I can't get a word from you. You don't seem to see me at all. What does it mean? Upon my soul, you terrify me with this deaf and dumb trick. What's going on in that head of yours? What are you plotting against me there so hard that you can't say a word? You will never make me believe that you – you – don't know where to lay your hands on a couple of hundred. You have made me curse the day I was born ...'

'Mr Massy,' said Captain Whalley, suddenly, without stirring.

The engineer started violently.

'If that is so I can only beg you to forgive me.'

'Starboard,' muttered the Serang to the helmsman; and the *Sofala* began to swing round the bend into the second reach.

'Ough!' Massy shuddered. 'You make my blood run cold. What made you come here? What made you come aboard that evening all of a sudden, with your high talk and your money – tempting me? I always wondered what was your motive? You fastened yourself on me to have easy times and grow fat on my life blood, I tell you. Was that it? I believe you are the greatest miser in the world, or else why ...'

'No. I am only poor,' interrupted Captain Whalley, stonily.

'Steady,' murmured the Serang. Massy turned away with his chin on his shoulder.

'I don't believe it,' he said in his dogmatic tone. Captain Whalley made no movement. 'There you sit like a gorged vulture – exactly like a vulture.'

He embraced the middle of the reach and both the banks in one blank, unseeing, circular glance, and left the bridge slowly.

9

ON turning to descend Massy perceived the head of Sterne the mate loitering, with his sly, confident smile, his red moustaches and blinking eyes, at the foot of the ladder.

Sterne had been a junior in one of the larger shipping concerns before joining the *Sofala*. He had thrown up his berth, he said, 'on general principle'. The promotion in the employ was very slow, he complained, and he thought it was time for him to try and get on a bit in the world. It seemed as though nobody would ever die or leave the firm; they all stuck fast in their berths till they got mildewed; he was tired of waiting; and he feared that when a vacancy did occur the best servants were by no means sure of being treated fairly. Besides, the captain he had to serve under – Captain Provost – was an unaccountable sort of man and had taken a dislike to him for some reason or other. For doing rather more than his bare duty as likely as not. When he had done anything wrong he could take a talking to, like a man; but he expected to be treated like a man, too, and not to be addressed invariably as though he were a dog. He had asked Captain Provost plump and plain to tell him where he was at fault, and Captain Provost, in a most scornful way, had told him that he was a perfect officer, and that if he disliked the way he was being spoken to there was the gangway – he could take himself off ashore at once. But everybody knew what sort of man Captain Provost was. It was no use appealing to the office. Captain Provost had too much influence in the employ. All the same, they had to give him a good character. He made bold to say there was nothing in the world against him, and, as he had happened

94

to hear that the mate of the *Sofala* had been taken to the hospital that morning with a sunstroke, he thought there would be no harm in seeing whether he would not do . . .

He had come to Captain Whalley freshly shaved, red-faced, thin-flanked, throwing out his lean chest; and had recited his little tale with an open and manly assurance. Now and then his eyelids quivered slightly, his hand would steal up to the end of the flaming moustache; his eyebrows were straight, furry, of a chestnut colour, and the directness of his gaze seemed to tremble on the verge of impudence. Captain Whalley had engaged him temporarily; then, the other man having been ordered home by the doctors, he had remained for the next trip, and then the next. He had now attained permanency, and the performance of his duties was marked by an air of serious, single-minded application. Directly he was spoken to, he began to smile attentively, with a great deference expressed in his whole attitude; but there was in the rapid winking which went on all the time something quizzical, as though he had possessed the secret of some universal joke cheating all creation and impenetrable to other mortals.

Grave and smiling he watched Massy come down step by step; when the chief engineer had reached the deck he swung about, and they found themselves face to face. Matched as to height and utterly dissimilar, they confronted each other as if there had been something between them — something else than the bright strip of sunlight that, falling through the wide lacing of two awnings, cut crosswise the narrow planking of the deck and separated their feet as it were a stream; something profound and subtle and incalculable, like an unexpressed understanding, a secret mistrust, or some sort of fear.

At last Sterne, blinking his deep-set eyes and sticking forward his scraped, clean-cut chin, as crimson as the rest of his face, murmured —

'You've seen? He grazed! You've seen?'

Massy, contemptuous, and without raising his yellow, fleshy countenance, replied in the same pitch —

'Maybe. But if it had been you we would have been stuck fast in the mud.'

'Pardon me, Mr Massy. I beg to deny it. Of course a shipowner may say what he jolly well pleases on his own deck. That's all right; but I beg to . . .'

'Get out of my way!'

The other had a slight start, the impulse of suppressed indignation perhaps, but held his ground. Massy's downward glance wandered right and left, as though the deck all round Sterne had been bestrewn with eggs that must not be broken, and he had looked irritably for places where he could set his feet in flight. In the end he, too, did not move, though there was plenty of room to pass on.

'I heard you say up there,' went on the mate – 'and a very just remark it was too – that there's always something wrong . . .'

'Eavesdropping is what's wrong with *you*, Mr Sterne.'

'Now, if you would only listen to me for a moment, Mr Massy, sir, I could . . .'

'You are a sneak,' interrupted Massy in a great hurry, and even managed to get so far as to repeat, 'a common sneak,' before the mate had broken in argumentatively –

'Now, sir, what is it you want? You want . . .'

'I want – I want,' stammered Massy, infuriated and astonished – 'I want? How do you know that I want anything? How dare you . . . What do you mean? . . . What are you after – you . . .'

'Promotion.' Sterne silenced him with candid bravado. The engineer's round soft cheeks quivered still, but he said quietly enough –

'You are only worrying my head off,' and Sterne met him with a confident little smile.

'A chap in business I know (well up in the world he is now) used to tell me that this was the proper way. "Always push on to the front," he would say. "Keep yourself well before your boss. Interfere whenever you get a chance. Show him what you know. Worry him into seeing you." That was his advice. Now I know no other boss than you here. You are the owner, and no one else counts for *that* much in my eyes. See, Mr Massy? I want to get on. I make no secret of it that I am one of the sort that means to get on. These are the men to make use of, sir. You haven't arrived at the top of the tree, sir, without finding that out – I daresay.'

'Worry your boss in order to get on,' repeated Massy, as if awestruck by the irreverent originality of the idea. 'I shouldn't wonder if this was just what the Blue Anchor people kicked you out of their employ for. Is that what you call getting on? You shall get on in the same way here if you aren't careful – I can promise you.'

At this Sterne hung his head, thoughtful, perplexed, winking hard at the deck. All his attempts to enter into confidential relations with his owner had led of late to nothing better than these dark threats of dismissal; and a threat of dismissal would check him at once into a hesitating silence as though he were not sure that the proper time for defying it had come. On this occasion he seemed to have lost his tongue for a moment, and Massy, getting in motion, heavily passed him by with an abortive attempt at shouldering. Sterne defeated it by stepping aside. He turned then swiftly, opening his mouth very wide as if to shout something after the engineer, but seemed to think better of it.

Always – as he was ready to confess – on the lookout for an opening to get on, it had become an instinct with him to watch the conduct of his immediate superiors for something 'that one could lay hold of'. It was his belief that no skipper in the world would keep his command for a day if only the owners could be 'made to know'. This romantic and naïve theory had led him into trouble more than once, but he remained incorrigible; and his character was so instinctively disloyal that whenever he joined a ship the intention of ousting his commander out of the berth and taking his place was always present at the back of his head, as a matter of course. It filled the leisure of his waking hours with the reveries of careful plans and compromising discoveries – the dreams of his sleep with images of lucky turns and favourable accidents. Skippers had been known to sicken and die at sea, than which nothing could be better to give a smart mate a chance of showing what he's made of. They also would tumble overboard sometimes: he had heard of one or two such cases. Others again ... But, as it were constitutionally, he was faithful to the belief that the conduct of no single one of them would stand the test of careful watching by a man who 'knew what's what' and who kept his eyes 'skinned pretty well' all the time.

After he had gained a permanent footing on board the *Sofala* he allowed his perennial hope to rise high. To begin with, it was a great advantage to have an old man for captain: the sort of man besides who in the nature of things was likely to give up the job before long from one cause or another. Sterne was greatly chagrined, however, to notice that he did not seem anyway near being past his work yet. Still, these old men go to pieces all at once sometimes. Then there was the owner-engineer close at hand to be impressed by his zeal and steadiness. Sterne never for a moment doubted the obvious nature of his own merits (he was really an excellent officer); only, nowadays, professional merit alone does not take a man along fast enough. A chap must have some push in him, and must keep his wits at work, too, to help him forward. He made up his mind to inherit the charge of this steamer if it was to be done at all; not indeed estimating the command of the *Sofala* as a very great catch, but for the reason that, out East especially, to make a start is everything, and one command leads to another.

He began by promising himself to behave with great circumspection; Massy's sombre and fantastic humours intimidated him as being outside one's usual sea experience; but he was quite intelligent enough to realize almost from the first that he was there in the presence of an exceptional situation. His peculiar prying imagination penetrated it quickly; the feeling that there was in it an element which eluded his grasp exasperated his impatience to get on. And so one trip came to an end, then another, and he had begun his third before he saw an opening by which he could step in with any sort of effect. It had all been very queer and very obscure; something had been going on near him, as if separated by a chasm from the common life and the working routine of the ship, which was exactly like the life and the routine of any other coasting steamer of that class.

Then one day he made his discovery.

It came to him after all these weeks of watchful observation and puzzled surmises, suddenly, like the long-sought solution of a riddle that suggests itself to the mind in a flash. Not with the same authority, however. Great heavens! Could it be that? And after remaining thunderstruck for a few seconds he tried to shake it off with self-contumely, as though it had been the product of an unhealthy bias towards the Incredible, the Inexplicable, the Unheard-of – the Mad!

This – the illuminating moment – had occurred the trip before, on the return passage. They had just left a place of call on the mainland called Pangu; they were steaming straight out of a bay. To the east a massive headland closed the view, with the tilted edges of the rocky strata showing through its ragged clothing of rank bushes and thorny creepers. The wind had begun to sing in the rigging; the sea along the coast, green and as if swollen a little above the line of the horizon, seemed to pour itself over, time after time, with a slow and thundering fall, into the shadow of the leeward cape; and across the wide opening the nearest of a group of small islands stood enveloped in the hazy yellow light of a breezy sunrise; still farther out the hummocky tops of other islets peeped out motionless above the water of the channels between, scoured tumultuously by the breeze.

The usual track of the *Sofala* both going and returning on every trip led her for a few miles along this reef-infested region. She followed a broad lane of water, dropping astern, one after another, these crumbs of the earth's crust resembling a squadron of dismasted hulks run in disorder upon a foul ground of rocks and shoals. Some of these fragments of land appeared, indeed, no bigger than a stranded ship; others, quite flat, lay awash like anchored rafts, like ponderous, black rafts of stone; several, heavily timbered and round at the base, emerged in squat domes of deep green foliage that shuddered darkly all over to the flying touch of cloud shadows driven by the sudden gusts of the squally season. The thunderstorms of the coast broke frequently over that cluster; it turned then shadowy in its whole extent; it turned more dark, and as if more still in the play of fire; as if more impenetrably silent in the peals of thunder; its blurred shapes vanished – dissolving utterly at times in the thick rain – to reappear clear-cut and black in the stormy light against the grey sheet of the cloud – scattered on the slaty round table of the sea. Unscathed by storms, resisting the work of years, unfretted by the strife of the world, there it lay unchanged as on that day, four hundred years ago, when first beheld by Western eyes from the deck of a high-pooped caravel.

It was one of these secluded spots that may be found on the

busy sea, as on land you come sometimes upon the clustered houses of a hamlet untouched by men's restlessness, untouched by their need, by their thought, and as if forgotten by time itself. The lives of uncounted generations had passed it by, and the multitudes of seafowl, urging their way from all the points of the horizon to sleep on the outer rocks of the group, unrolled the converging evolutions of their flight in long, sombre streamers upon the glow of the sky. The palpitating cloud of their wings soared and stooped over the pinnacles of the rocks, over the rocks slender like spires, squat like martello towers; over the pyramidal heaps like fallen ruins, over the lines of bald boulders showing like a wall of stones battered to pieces and scorched by lightning – with the sleepy, clear glimmer of water in every breach. The noise of their continuous and violent screaming filled the air.

This great noise would meet the *Sofala* coming up from Batu Beru; it would meet her on quiet evenings, a pitiless and savage clamour enfeebled by distance, the clamour of seabirds settling to rest, and struggling for a footing at the end of the day. No one noticed it especially on board; it was the voice of their ship's unerring landfall, ending the steady stretch of a hundred miles. She had made good her course, she had run her distance till the punctual islets began to emerge one by one, the points of rocks, the hummocks of earth ... and the cloud of birds hovered – the restless cloud emitting a strident and cruel uproar, the sound of the familiar scene, the living part of the broken land beneath, of the outspread sea, and of the high sky without a flaw.

But when the *Sofala* happened to close with the land after sunset she would find everything very still there under the mantle of the night. All would be still, dumb, almost invisible – but for the blotting out of the low constellations occulted in turns behind the vague masses of the islets whose true outlines eluded the eye amongst the dark spaces of the heaven: and the ship's three lights, resembling three stars – the red and the green with the white above – her three lights, like three companion stars wandering on the earth, held their unswerving course for the passage at the southern end of the group. Sometimes there were human eyes open to watch them come nearer, travelling smoothly in the sombre void; the eyes of a naked fisherman in his canoe floating over a reef. He thought drowsily: 'Ho! The fire-ship that once in every moon goes in and comes out of Pangu Bay.' More he did not know of her. And just as he had detected the faint rhythm of the propeller beating the calm water a mile and a half away, the time would come for the *Sofala* to altar her course, the lights would swing off him their triple beam – and disappear.

A few miserable, half-naked families, a sort of outcast tribe of long-haired, lean, and wild-eyed people, strove for their living in this lonely wilderness of islets, lying like an abandoned outwork of the land at the gates of the bay. Within the knots and loops of the rocks the water rested more transparent than crystal under their crooked and leaky canoes, scooped out of the trunk of a tree: the forms of the bottom undulated slightly to the dip of a paddle; and the men seemed to hang in the air, they seemed to hang enclosed within the fibres of a dark, sodden log, fishing patiently in a strange, unsteady, pellucid, green air above the shoals.

Their bodies stalked brown and emaciated as if dried up in the sunshine; their lives ran out silently; the homes where they were born, went to rest, and died – flimsy sheds of rushes and coarse grass eked out with a few ragged mats – were hidden out of sight from the open sea. No glow of their household fires ever kindled for a seaman a red spark upon the blind night of the group: and the calms of the coast, the flaming long calms of the equator, the unbreathing, concentrated calms like the deep introspection of a passionate nature, brooded awfully for days and weeks, together over the unchangeable inheritance of their children; till at last the stones, hot like live embers, scorched the naked sole, till the water clung warm, and sickly, and as if thickened about the legs of lean men with girded loins, wading thigh-deep in the pale blaze of the shallows. And it would happen now and then that the *Sofala*, through some delay in one of the ports of call, would heave in sight making for Pangu Bay as late as noonday.

Only a blurring cloud at first, the thin mist of her smoke would arise mysteriously from an empty point on the clear line of sea and sky. The taciturn fishermen within the reefs would extend their lean arms towards the offing; and the brown figures stooping on the tiny beaches, the brown figures of men, women, and children grubbing in the sand in search of turtles' eggs, would rise up, crooked elbow aloft and hand over the eyes, to watch this monthly apparition glide straight on, swerve on – and go by. Their ears caught the panting of that ship; their eyes followed her till she passed between the two capes of the mainland going at full speed as though she hoped to make her way unchecked into the very bosom of the earth.

On such days the luminous sea would give no sign of the dangers lurking on both sides of her path. Everything remained still, crushed by the overwhelming power of the light; and the whole group, opaque in the sunshine, – the rocks resembling pinnacles, the rocks resembling spires, the rocks resembling ruins; the forms of islets resembling beehives, resembling mole-hills; the islets recalling the shapes of haystacks, the contours of ivy-clad towers – would stand reflected together upside down in the unwrinkled water, like carved toys of ebony disposed on the silvered plate-glass of a mirror.

The first touch of blowing weather would envelop the whole at once in the spume of the windward breakers, as if in a sudden cloudlike burst of steam; and the clear water seemed fairly to boil in all the passages. The provoked sea outlined exactly in a design of angry foam the wide base of the group; the submerged level of broken waste and refuse left over from the building of the coast near by, projecting its dangerous spurs, all awash, far into the channel, and bristling with wicked long spits often a mile long: with deadly spits made of froth and stones.

And even nothing more than a brisk breeze – as on that morning, the voyage before, when the *Sofala* left Pangu Bay early, and Mr Sterne's discovery was to blossom out like a flower of incredible and evil aspect from the tiny seed of instinctive suspicion – even such a breeze had enough strength to tear the placid mask from the face of the sea. To Sterne, gazing with indifference, it had been like a revelation to behold for the first time the dangers marked by the hissing livid patches on the water as distinctly as on the engraved paper of a chart. It came into his mind that this was the sort of day most favourable for a stranger attempting the passage: a clear day, just windy enough for the sea to break on every ledge, buoying, as it were, the channel plainly to the sight; whereas during a calm you had nothing to depend on but the compass and the practised judgement of your eye. And yet the successive captains of the *Sofala* had had to take her through at night more than once. Nowadays you could not afford to throw away six or seven hours of a steamer's time. That you couldn't. But then use is everything, and with proper care ... The channel was broad and safe enough; the main point was to hit upon the entrance correctly in the dark — for if a man got himself involved in that stretch of broken water over yonder he would never get out with a whole ship — if he ever got out at all.

This was Sterne's last train of thought independent of the great discovery. He had just seen to the securing of the anchor, and had remained forward idling away a moment or two. The captain was in charge on the bridge. With a slight yawn he had turned away from his survey of the sea and had leaned his shoulders against the fish davit.

These, properly speaking, were the very last moments of ease he was to know on board the *Sofala*. All the instants that came after were to be pregnant with purpose and intolerable with perplexity. No more idle, random thoughts; the discovery would put them on the rack, till sometimes he wished to goodness he had been fool enough not to make it at all. And yet, if his chance to get on rested on the discovery of 'something wrong', he could not have hoped for a greater stroke of luck.

10

THE knowledge was too disturbing, really. There was 'something wrong' with a vengeance, and the moral certitude of it was at first simply frightful to contemplate. Sterne had been looking aft in a mood so idle, that for once he was thinking no harm of any one. His captain on the bridge presented himself naturally to his sight. How insignificant, how casual was the thought that had started the train of discovery — like an accidental spark that suffices to ignite the charge of a tremendous mine!

Caught under by the breeze, the awnings of the foredeck bellied upwards and collapsed slowly, and above their heavy flapping the grey stuff of Captain Whalley's roomy coat fluttered incessantly around his arms and trunk. He faced the wind in full light, with his great silvery beard blown forcibly against his chest; the eyebrows overhung heavily the shadows whence his glance appeared to be staring ahead piercingly. Sterne could just detect the twin gleam of the whites shifting under the shaggy arches of the brow. At short range these eyes, for all the man's affable manner, seemed to look you through and through. Sterne never could defend himself from that feeling when he had occasion to speak with his captain. He did not like it. What a big heavy man he appeared up there, with that little shrimp of a Serang in close attendance – as was usual in this extraordinary steamer! Confounded absurd custom that. He resented it. Surely the old fellow could have looked after his ship without that loafing native at his elbow. Sterne wriggled his shoulders with disgust. What was it? Indolence or what?

That old skipper must have been growing lazy for years. They all grew lazy out East here (Sterne was very conscious of his own unimpaired activity); they got slack all over. But he towered very erect on the bridge; and quite low by his side, as you see a small child looking over the edge of a table, the battered soft hat and the brown face of the Serang peeped over the white canvas screen of the rail.

No doubt the Malay was standing back, nearer to the wheel; but the great disparity of size in close association amused Sterne like the observation of a bizarre fact in nature. There were as queer fish out of the sea as any in it.

He saw Captain Whalley turn his head quickly to speak to his Serang; the wind whipped the whole white mass of the beard sideways. He would be directing the chap to look at the compass for him, or what not. Of course. Too much trouble to step over and see for himself. Sterne's scorn for that bodily indolence which overtakes white men in the East increased on reflection. Some of them would be utterly lost if they hadn't all these natives at their beck and call; they grew perfectly shameless about it, too. He was not of that sort, thank God! It wasn't in him to make himself dependent for his work on any shrivelled-up little Malay like that. As if one could ever trust a silly native for anything in the world! But that fine old man thought differently, it seems.

There they were together, never far apart; a pair of them, recall-ing to the mind an old whale attended by a little pilot-fish.

The fancifulness of the comparison made him smile, A whale with an inseparable pilot-fish! That's what the old man looked like; for it could not be said he looked like a shark, though Mr Massy had called him that very name. But Mr Massy did not mind what he said in his savage fits. Sterne smiled to himself – and gradually the ideas evoked by the sound, by the imagined shape of the word pilot-fish; the ideas of aid, of guidance needed and received, came uppermost in his mind: the word pilot awak-ened the idea of trust, of dependence, the idea of the welcome, clear-eyed help brought to the seaman groping for the land in the dark: groping blindly in fogs: feeling his way in the thick weather of the gales that, filling the air with a salt mist blown up from the sea, contract the range of sight on all sides to a shrunken horizon that seems within reach of the hand.

A pilot sees better than a stranger, because his local know-ledge, like a sharper vision, completes the shapes of things hur-riedly glimpsed; penetrates the veils of mist spread over the land by the storms of the sea; defines with certitude the outlines of a coast lying under the pall of fog, the forms of landmarks half buried in a starless night as in a shallow grave. He recognizes because he already knows. It is not to his far-reaching eye but to his more extensive knowledge that the pilot looks for certitudes; for this certitude of the ship's position on which may depend a man's good fame and the peace of his conscience, the justifica-tion of the trust deposited in his hands, with his own life, too, which is seldom wholly his to throw away, and the humble lives of others rooted in distant affections, perhaps, and made as weighty as the lives of kings by the burden of the awaiting mystery. The pilot's knowledge brings relief and certitude to the commander of a ship; the Serang, however, in his fanciful sug-gestion of a pilot-fish attending a whale, could not in any way be credited with a superior knowledge. Why should he have it? These two men had come on that run together – the white and the brown – on the same day: and of course a white man would learn more in a week than the best native would in a month. He was made to stick to the skipper as though he were of some use – as the pilot-fish, they say, is to the whale. But how – it was very marked – how? A pilot-fish – a pilot – a ... But if not superior knowledge then ...

Sterne's discovery was made. It was repugnant to his imagination, shocking to his ideas of honesty, shocking to his conception of mankind. This enormity affected one's outlook on what was possible in this world: it was as if for instance the sun had turned blue, throwing a new and sinister light on men and nature. Really in the first moment he had felt sickish, as though he had got a blow below the belt: for a second the very colour of the sea seemed changed – appeared queer to his wandering eye; and he had a passing, unsteady sensation in all his limbs as though the earth had started turning the other way.

A very natural incredulity succeeding this sense of upheaval brought a measure of relief. He had gasped; it was over. But afterwards, during all that day, sudden paroxysms of wonder would come over him in the midst of his occupations. He would stop and shake his head. The revolt of his incredulity had passed away almost as quick as the first emotion of discovery, and for the next twenty-four hours he had no sleep. That would never do. At meal-times (he took the foot of the table set up for the white men on the bridge) he could not help losing himself in a fascinated contemplation of Captain Whalley opposite. He watched the deliberate upward movements of the arm; the old man put his food to his lips as though he never expected to find any taste in his daily bread, as though he did not know anything about it. He fed himself like a somnambulist. 'It's an awful sight,' thought Sterne; and he watched the long period of mournful, silent immobility, with a big brown hand lying loosely closed by the side of the plate, till he noticed the two engineers to the right and left looking at him in astonishment. He would close his mouth in a hurry then, and lowering his eyes, wink rapidly at his plate. It was awful to see the old chap sitting there: it was even awful to think that with three words he could blow him up sky-high. All he had to do was to raise his voice and pronounce a single short sentence, and yet that simple act seemed as impossible to attempt as moving the sun out of its place in the sky. The old chap could eat in his terrific mechanical way; but Sterne, from mental excitement, could not – not that evening, at any rate.

He had had ample time since to get accustomed to the strain of the meal-hours. He would never have believed it. But then use is everything; only the very potency of his success prevented anything resembling elation. He felt like a man who, in his legitimate search for a loaded gun to help him on his way through the world, chances to come upon a torpedo – upon a live torpedo with a shattering charge in its head and a pressure of many atmospheres in its tail. It is the sort of weapon to make its possessor careworn and nervous. He had no mind to be blown up himself; and he could not get rid of the notion that the explosion was bound to damage him, too, in some way.

This vague apprehension had restrained him at first. He was able now to eat and sleep with that fearful weapon by his side, with the conviction of its power always in his mind. It had not been arrived at by any reflective process; but once the idea had entered his head, the conviction had followed overwhelmingly in a multitude of observed little facts to which before he had given only a languid attention. The abrupt and faltering intonations of the deep voice; the taciturnity put on like an armour; the deliberate, as if guarded, movements; the long immobilities, as if the man he watched had been afraid to disturb the very air: every familiar gesture, every word uttered in his hearing, every sigh overheard, had acquired a special significance, a confirmatory import.

Every day that passed over the *Sofala* appeared to Sterne simply crammed full with proofs – with incontrovertible proofs. At night, when off duty, he would steal out of his cabin in pyjamas (for more proofs) and stand a full hour, perhaps, on his bare feet below the bridge, as absolutely motionless as the awning stanchion in its deck socket near by. On the stretches of easy navigation it is not usual for a coasting captain to remain on deck all the time of his watch. The Serang keeps it for him as a matter of custom; in open water, on a straight course, he is usually trusted to look after the ship by himself. But this old man seemed incapable of remaining quietly down below. No doubt he could not sleep. And no wonder. This was also a proof. Suddenly in the silence of the ship panting upon the still, dark sea, Sterne would hear a low voice above him exclaiming nervously –

'Serang!'

'Tuan!'

'You are watching the compass well?'

'Yes, I am watching, Tuan.'

'The ship is making her course?'

'She is, Tuan. Very straight.'

'It is well; and remember, Serang, that the order is, that you are to mind the helmsmen and keep a lookout with care, the same as if I were not on deck.'

Then, when the Serang had made his answer, the low tones on the bridge would cease, and everything round Sterne seemed to become more still and more profoundly silent. Silently chilled and with his back aching a little from long immobility, he would steal away to his room on the port side of the deck. He had long since parted with the last vestige of incredulity; of the original emotions, set into a tumult by the discovery, some trace of the first awe alone remained. Not the awe of the man himself – he could blow him up sky-high with six words – rather it was an awestruck indignation at the reckless perversity of avarice (what else could it be?), at the mad and sombre resolution that for the sake of a few dollars more seemed to set at nought the common rule of conscience and pretended to struggle against the very decree of Providence.

You could not find another man like this one in the whole round world – thank God. There was something devilishly dauntless in the character of such a deception which made you pause.

Other considerations occurring to his prudence had kept him tongue-tied from day to day. It seemed to him now that it would yet have been easier to speak out in the first hour of discovery. He almost regretted not having made a row at once. But then the very monstrosity of the disclosure ... Why! he could hardly face it himself, let alone pointing it out to somebody else. Moreover, with a desperado of that sort one never knew. The object was not to get him out (that was as well as done already), but to step into his place. Bizarre as the thought seemed he might have shown fight. A fellow up to working such a fraud would have enough cheek for anything; a fellow that, as it were, stood up against God Almighty Himself. He was a horrid marvel –

that's what he was: he was perfectly capable of brazening out the affair scandalously till he got him (Sterne) kicked out of the ship and everlastingly damaged his prospects in this part of the East. Yet if you want to get on something must be risked. At times Sterne thought he had been unduly timid of taking action in the past; and what was worse, it had come to this, that in the present he did not seem to know what action to take.

Massy's savage moroseness was too disconcerting. It was an incalculable factor of the situation. You could not tell what there was behind that insulting ferocity. How could one trust such a temper? it did not put Sterne in bodily fear for himself, but it frightened him exceedingly as to his prospects.

Though of course inclined to credit himself with exceptional powers of observation, he had by now lived too long with his discovery. He had gone on looking at nothing else, till at last one day it occurred to him that the thing was so obvious that no one could miss seeing it. There were four white men in all on board the *Sofala*. Jack, the second engineer, was too dull to notice anything that took place out of his engine-room. Remained Massy – the owner – the interested person – nearly going mad with worry. Sterne had heard and seen more than enough on board to know what ailed him; but his exasperation seemed to make him deaf to cautious overtures. If he had only known it, there was the very thing he wanted. But how could you bargain with a man of that sort? It was like going into a tiger's den with a piece of raw meat in your hand. He was as likely as not to rend you for your pains. In fact, he was always threatening to do that very thing; and the urgency of the case, combined with the impossibility of handling it with safety, made Sterne in his watches below toss and mutter open-eyed in his bunk, for hours, as though he had been burning with fever.

Occurrences like the crossing of the bar just now were extremely alarming to his prospects. He did not want to be left behind by some swift catastrophe. Massy being on the bridge, the old man had to brace himself up, and make a show, he supposed. But it was getting very bad with him, very bad indeed, now. Even Massy had been emboldened to find fault this time; Sterne, listening at the foot of the ladder, had heard the other's whimpering and artless denunciations. Luckily the beast was very stupid and could not see the why of all this. However, small blame to him; it took a clever man to hit upon the cause. Nevertheless, it was high time to do something. The old man's game could not be kept up for many days more.

'I may yet lose my life at this fooling – let alone my chance,' Sterne mumbled angrily to himself, after the stooping back of the chief engineer had disappeared round the corner of the skylight. Yes, no doubt – he thought; but to blurt out his knowledge would not advance his prospects. On the contrary, it would blast them utterly as likely as not. He dreaded another failure. He had a vague consciousness of not being much liked by his fellows in this part of the world; inexplicably enough, for he had done nothing to them. Envy, he supposed. People were always down on a clever chap who made no bones about his determination to get on. To do your duty and count on the gratitude of that brute Massy would be sheer folly. He was a bad lot. Unmanly! A vicious man! Bad! Bad! A brute! A brute without a spark of anything human about him; without so much as simple curiosity even, or else surely he would have responded in some way to all these hints he had been given ... Such insensibility was almost mysterious. Massy's state of exasperation seemed to Sterne to have made him stupid beyond the ordinary silliness of shipowners.

Sterne, meditating on the embarrassments of that stupidity, forgot himself completely. His stony, unwinking stare was fixed on the planks of the deck.

The slight quiver agitating the whole fabric of the ship was more perceptible in the silent river, shaded and still like a forest path. The *Sofala*, gliding with an even motion, had passed beyond the coast-belt of mud and mangroves. The shores rose higher, in firm sloping banks, and the forest of big trees came down to the brink. Where the earth had been crumbled by the floods it showed a steep brown cut, denuding a mass of roots intertwined as if wrestling underground; and in the air, the interlaced boughs, bound and loaded with creepers, carried on the struggle for life, mingled their foliage in one solid wall of leaves, with here and there the shape of an enormous dark pillar soaring, or a ragged opening, as if torn by the flight of a cannonball, disclosing the impenetrable gloom within, the secular inviolable shade of the virgin forest. The thump of the engines reverberated like the strokes of a metronome beating the measure of the vast silence, the shadow of the western wall had fallen across the river, and the smoke pouring backwards from the funnel eddied down behind the ship, spread a thin dusky veil over the sombre water, which, checked by the flood-tide, seemed to lie stagnant in the whole straight length of the reaches.

Sterne's body, as if rooted on the spot, trembled slightly from top to toe with the internal vibration of the ship; from under his feet came sometimes a sudden clang of iron, the noisy burst of a shout below; to the right the leaves of the tree-tops caught the rays of the low sun, and seemed to shine with a golden green light of their own shimmering around the highest boughs which stood out black against a smooth blue sky that seemed to droop over the bed of the river like the roof of a tent. The passengers for Batu Beru, kneeling on the planks, were engaged in rolling their bedding of mats busily; they tied up bundles, they snapped the locks of wooden chests. A pockmarked pedlar of small wares threw his head back to drain into his throat the last drops out of an earthenware bottle before putting it away in a roll of blankets. Knots of travelling traders standing about the deck conversed in low tones; the followers of a small Rajah from down the coast, broad-faced simple young fellows in white drawers and round white cotton caps with their coloured sarongs twisted across their bronze shoulders, squatted on their hams on the hatch, chewing betel with bright red mouths as if they had been tasting blood. Their spears, lying piled up together within the circle of their bare toes, resembled a casual bundle of dry bamboos; a thin, livid Chinaman, with a bulky package wrapped up in leaves already thrust under his arm, gazed ahead eagerly; a wandering King rubbed his teeth with a bit of wood, pouring over the side a bright stream of water out of his lips; the fat Rajah dozed in a shabby deckchair – and at the turn of every bend the two walls of leaves reappeared running parallel along the banks, with their impenetrable solidity fading at the top to a vaporous mistiness of countless slender twigs growing free, of young delicate branches shooting from the topmost limbs of hoary trunks, of feathery heads of climbers like delicate silver sprays standing up without a quiver. There was not a sign of a clearing anywhere; not a trace of human habitation, except when in one place, on the bare end of a low point under an isolated group of slender tree-ferns, the jagged, tangled remnants of an old hut on piles appeared with that peculiar aspect of ruined bamboo walls that look as if smashed with a club. Farther on, half hidden under the drooping bushes, a canoe containing a man and a woman together with a dozen green cocoanuts in a heap, rocked helplessly after the *Sofala* had passed, like a navigating contrivance of venturesome insects, of travelling ants; while two glassy folds of water streaming away from each bow of the steamer across the whole width of the river ran with her upstream smoothly, fretting their outer ends into a brown whispering tumble of froth against the miry foot of each bank.

'I must,' thought Sterne, 'bring that brute .Massy to his bearings. It's getting too absurd in the end. Here's the old man up there buried in his chair – he may just as well be in his grave for all the use he'll ever be in the world – and the Serang's in charge. Because that's what he is. In charge. In the place that's mine by rights. I must bring that savage brute to his bearings. I'll do it at once, too . . .'

When the mate made an abrupt start, a little brown, half-naked boy, with large black eyes, and the string of a written charm round his neck, became panic-struck at once. He dropped the banana he had been munching, and ran to the knee of a grave dark Arab in flowing robes, sitting like a Biblical figure, incongruously, on a yellow tin trunk corded with a rope of twisted rattan. The father, unmoved, put out his hand to pat the little shaven poll protectingly.

II

STERNE crossed the deck upon the track of the chief engineer. Jack, the second, retreating backwards down the engine-room ladder, and still wiping his hands, treated him to an incomprehensible grin of white teeth out of his grimy hard face; Massy was nowhere to be seen. Sterne scratched at the door softly, then, putting his lips to the rose of the ventilator, said –

'I must speak to you, Mr Massy. Just give me a minute or two.'

'I am busy. Go away from my door.'

'But pray, Mr Massy . . .'

'You go away. D'you hear? Take yourself off altogether — to the other end of the ship — quite away . . .' The voice inside dropped low. 'To the devil.'

Sterne paused : then very quietly —

'It's rather pressing. When do you think you will be at liberty, sir?'

The answer to this was an exasperated 'Never'; and at once Sterne, with a very firm expression of face, turned the handle.

Mr Massy's stateroom — a narrow, one-berth cabin — smelt strongly of soap, and presented to view a swept, dusted, un-adorned neatness, not so much bare as barren, not so much severe as starved and lacking in humanity, like the ward of a public hospital, or rather (owing to the small size) like the clean retreat of a desperately poor but exemplary person. Not a single photograph frame ornamented the bulk-heads; not a single article of clothing, not as much as a spare cap, hung from the brass hooks. All the inside was painted in one plain tint of pale blue; two big sea-chests in sailcloth covers and with iron padlocks fitted exactly in the space under the bunk. One glance was enough to embrace all the strip of scrubbed planks within the four unconcealed corners. The absence of the usual settee was striking; the teak-wood top of the washing-stand seemed herme-tically closed, and so was the lid of the writing-desk, which pro-truded from the partition at the foot of the bed-place, containing a mattress as thin as a pancake under a threadbare blanket with a faded red stripe, and a folded mosquito-net against the nights spent in harbour. There was not a scrap of paper anywhere in sight, no boots on the floor, no litter of any sort, not a speck of dust anywhere; no traces of pipe-ash even, which, in a heavy smoker, was morally revolting, like a manifestation of extreme hypocrisy; and the bottom of the old wooden arm-chair (the only seat there), polished with much use, shone as if its shabbi-ness had been waxed. The screen of leaves on the bank, passing as if unrolled endlessly in the round opening of the port, sent a wavering network of light and shade into the place.

Sterne, holding the door open with one hand, had thrust in his head and shoulders. At this amazing intrusion Massy, who was doing absolutely nothing, jumped up speechless.

'Don't call names,' murmured Sterne, hurriedly. 'I won't be called names. I think of nothing but your good, Mr Massy.'

A pause as of extreme astonishment followed. They both seemed to have lost their tongues. Then the mate went on with discreet glibness:

'You simply couldn't conceive what's going on on board your ship. It wouldn't enter your head for a moment. You are too good – too – too upright, Mr Massy, to suspect anybody of such a ... It's enough to make your hair stand on end.'

He watched for the effect: Massy seemed dazed, uncomprehending. He only passed the palm of his hand on the coal-black wisps plastered across the top of his head. In a tone suddenly changed to confidential audacity Sterne hastened on:

'Remember that there's only six weeks left to run ...' The other was looking at him stonily ... 'So anyhow you will require a captain for the ship before long.'

Then only, as if that suggestion had scarified his flesh in the manner of red-hot iron, Massy gave a start and seemed ready to shriek. He contained himself by a great effort.

'Require – a – captain,' he repeated with scathing slowness. 'Who requires a captain? You dare tell me that I need any of you humbugging sailors to run my ship. You and your likes have been fattening on me for years. It would have hurt me less to throw my money overboard. Pam – pe – red us – e – less f-f-f-frauds. The old ship knows as much as the best of you.' He snapped his teeth audibly and growled through them. 'The silly law requires a captain.'

Sterne had taken heart of grace meantime.

'And the silly insurance people, too, as well,' he said, lightly. 'But never mind that. What I want to ask is: Why shouldn't *I* do, sir? I don't say but you could take a steamer about the world as well as any of us sailors. I don't pretend to tell *you* that it is a very great trick ...' He emitted a short, hollow guffaw, familiarly '... I didn't make the law – but there it is; and I am an active young fellow; I quite hold with your ideas; I know your ways by this time, Mr Massy. I wouldn't try to give myself airs like that – that – er – lazy specimen of an old man up there.'

He put a marked emphasis on the last sentence, to lead Massy away from the track in case ... but he did not doubt of now holding his success. The chief engineer seemed nonplussed, like a slow man invited to catch hold of a whirligig of some sort.

'What you want, sir, is a chap with no nonsense about him, who would be content to be your sailing-master. Quite right, too. Well, I am fit for the work as much as that Serang. Because that's what it amounts to. Do you know, sir, that a dam' Malay like a monkey is in charge of your ship – and no one else? Just listen to his feet pit-patting above us on the bridge – real officer in charge. He's taking her up the river while the great man is wallowing in the chair – perhaps asleep; and if he is, that would not make it much worse either – take my word for it.'

He tried to thrust himself farther in. Massy, with lowered forehead, one hand grasping the back of the arm-chair, did not budge.

'You think, sir, that the man has got you tight in his agreement ...' Massy raised a heavy snarling face at this ... 'Well, sir, one can't help hearing of it on board. It's no secret. And it has been the talk on shore for years; fellows have been making bets about it. No, sir! It's *you* who have got him at your mercy. You will say that you can't dismiss him for indolence. Difficult to prove in court, and so on. Why, yes. But if you say the word, sir, I can tell you something about his indolence that will give you the clear right to fire him out on the spot and put me in charge for the rest of this very trip – yes, sir, before we leave Batu Beru – and make him pay a dollar a day for his keep till we get back, if you like. Now, what do you think of that? Come, sir. Say the word. It's really well worth your while, and I am quite ready to take your bare word. A definite statement from you would be as good as a bond.'

His eyes began to shine. He insisted. A simple statement – and he thought to himself that he would manage somehow to stick in his berth as long as it suited him. He would make himself indispensable; the ship had a bad name in her port; it would be easy to scare the fellows off. Massy would have to keep him.

'A definite statement from me would be enough,' Massy repeated, slowly.

'Yes, sir. It would.' Sterne stuck out his chin cheerily and blinked at close quarters with that unconscious impudence which had the power to enrage Massy beyond anything.

The engineer spoke very distinctly:

'Listen well to me, then, Mr Sterne: I wouldn't – d'ye hear? – I wouldn't promise you the value of two pence for anything *you* can tell me.'

He struck Sterne's arm away with a smart blow, and catching hold of the handle pulled the door to. The terrific slam darkened the cabin instantaneously to his eyes as if after the flash of an explosion. At once he dropped into the chair. 'Oh, no! You don't!' he whispered faintly.

The ship had in that place to shave the bank so close that the gigantic wall of leaves came gliding like a shutter against the port; the darkness of the primeval forest seemed to flow into that bare cabin with the odour of rotting leaves, of sodden soil – the strong muddy smell of the living earth steaming uncovered after the passing of a deluge. The bushes swished loudly alongside; above there was a series of crackling sounds, with a sharp rain of small broken branches falling on the bridge; a creeper with a great rustle snapped on the head of a boat davit, and a long, luxuriant green twig actually whipped in and out of the open port, leaving behind a few torn leaves that remained suddenly at rest on Mr Massy's blanket. Then, the ship sheering out in the stream, the light began to return, but did not augment beyond a subdued clearness: for the sun was very low already, and the river, wending its sinuous course through a multitude of secular trees as if at the bottom of a precipitous gorge, had been already invaded by a deepening gloom – the swift precursor of the night.

'Oh, no, you don't!' murmured the engineer again. His lips trembled almost imperceptibly; his hands, too, a little: and to calm himself he opened the writing-desk, spread out a sheet of thin greyish paper covered with a mass of printed figures and began to scan them attentively for the twentieth time this trip at least.

With his elbows propped, his head between his hands, he seemed to lose himself in the study of an abstruse problem in mathematics. It was the list of the winning numbers from the last drawing of the great lottery which had been the one inspiring fact of so many years of his existence. The conception of a life deprived of that periodical sheet of paper had slipped away from him entirely, as another man, according to his nature, would not have been able to conceive a world without fresh air, without activity, or without affection. A great pile of flimsy sheets had been growing for years in his desk, while the *Sofala*, driven by the faithful Jack, wore out her boilers in tramping up and down the Straits, from cape to cape, from river to river, from bay to bay; accumulating by that hard labour of an overworked, starved ship the blackened mass of these documents. Massy kept them under lock and key like a treasure. There was in them, as in the experience of life, the fascination of hope, the excitement of a half-penetrated mystery, the longing of a half-satisfied desire.

For days together, on a trip, he would shut himself up in his berth with them: the thump of the toiling engines pulsated in his ear; and he would weary his brain poring over the rows of disconnected figures, bewildering by their senseless sequence, resembling the hazards of destiny itself. He nourished a conviction that there must be some logic lurking somewhere in the results of change. He thought he had seen its very form. His head swam; his limbs ached; he puffed at his pipe mechanically; a contemplative stupor would soothe the fretfulness of his temper, like the passive bodily quietude procured by a drug, while the intellect remains tensely on the stretch. Nine, nine, nought, four, two. He made a note. The next winning number of the great prize was forty-seven thousand and five. These numbers of course would have to be avoided in the future when writing to Manila for the tickets. He mumbled, pencil in hand ... 'and five. Hm ... hm.' He wetted his finger: the papers rustled. Ha! But what's this? Three years ago, in the September drawing, it was number nine, nought, four, two that took the first prize. Most remarkable. There was a hint there of a definite rule! He was afraid of missing some recondite principle in the overwhelming wealth of his material. What could it be? and for half an hour he would remain dead still, bent low over the desk, without twitching a muscle. At his back the whole berth would be thick with a heavy body of smoke, as if a bomb had burst in there, unnoticed, unheard.

At last he would lock up the desk with the decision of un-shaken confidence, jump up and go out. He would walk swiftly back and forth on that part of the foredeck which was kept clear of the lumber and of the bodies of the native passengers. They were a great nuisance, but they were also a source of pro-fit that could not be disdained. He needed every penny of profit the *Sofala* could make. Little enough it was, in all conscience! The incertitude of chance gave him no concern, since he had somehow arrived at the conviction that, in the course of years, every number was bound to have its winning turn. It was simply a matter of time and of taking as many tickets as he could afford for every drawing. He generally took rather more; all the earn-ings of the ship went that way, and also the wages he allowed himself as chief engineer. It was the wages he paid to others that he begrudged with a reasoned and at the same time a passionate regret. He scowled at the lascars with their deck brooms, at the quartermasters rubbing the brass rails with greasy rags; he was eager to shake his fist and roar abuse in bad Malay at the poor carpenter – a timid, sickly, opium-fuddled Chinaman, in loose blue drawers for all costume, who invariably dropped his tools and fled below, with streaming tail and shaking all over, before the fury of that 'devil'. But it was when he raised up his eyes to the bridge where one of these sailor frauds was always planted by law in charge of his ship that he felt almost dizzy with rage. He abominated them all; it was an old feud, from the time he first went to sea, an unlicked cub with a great opinion of himself, in the engine-room. The slights that had been put upon him. The persecutions he had suffered at the hands of skippers – of absolute nobodies in a steamship after all. And now that he had risen to be a shipowner they were still a plague to him: he had absolutely to pay away precious money to the conceited useless loafers: – As if a fully qualified engineer – who was the owner as well – were not fit to be trusted with the whole charge of a ship. Well! he made it pretty warm for them; but it was a poor consolation. He had come in time to hate the ship, too, for the repairs she required, for the coal-bills he had to pay, for the poor beggarly freights she earned. He would clench his hand as he walked and hit the rail a sudden blow, viciously, as though she could be made to feel pain. And yet he could not do without her; he needed her; he must hang on to her tooth and nail to keep his head above water till the expected flood of fortune came sweeping up and landed him safely on the high shore of his ambition.

It was now to do nothing, nothing whatever, and have plenty of money to do it on. He had tasted of power, the highest form of it his limited experience was aware of – the power of ship-owning. What a deception! Vanity of vanities! He wondered at his folly. He had thrown away the substance for the shadow. Of the gratification of wealth he did not know enough to excite his imagination with any visions of luxury. How could he – the child of a drunken boiler-maker – going straight from the work-shop into the engine-room of a north-country collier! But the notion of the absolute idleness of wealth he could very well con-ceive. He revelled in it, to forget his present troubles; he im-agined himself walking about the streets of Hull (he knew their gutters well as a boy) with his pockets full of sovereigns. He would buy himself a house; his married sisters, their husbands, his old workshop chums, would render him infinite homage. There would be nothing to think of. His word would be law. He had been out of work for a long time before he won his prize, and he remembered how Carlo Mariani (commonly known as Paunchy Charley), the Maltese hotel-keeper at the slummy end of Denham Street, had cringed joyfully before him in the even-ing, when the news had come. Poor Charley, though he made his living by ministering to various abject vices, gave credit for the food to many a piece of white wreckage. He was naïvely overjoyed at the idea of his old bills being paid, and he reckoned confidently on a spell of festivities in the cavernous grog-shop downstairs. Massy remembered the curious, respectful looks of the 'trashy' white men in the place. His heart had swelled within him. Massy had left Charley's infamous den directly he had realized the possibilities open to him, with his nose in the air. Afterwards the memory of these adulations was a great sadness.

This was the true power of money – and no trouble with it, nor any thinking required either. He thought with difficulty and felt vividly; to his blunt brain the problems offered by any ordered scheme of life seemed in their cruel toughness to have been put in his way by the obvious malevolence of men. As a shipowner everyone had conspired to make him a nobody. How could he have been such a fool as to purchase that accursed ship? He had been abominably swindled; there was no end to this swindling, and as the difficulties of his improvident ambition gathered thicker round him, he really came to hate everybody he had ever come in contact with. A temper naturally irritable and an amazing sensitiveness to the claims of his own personality had ended by making of life for him a sort of inferno – a place where his lost soul had been given up to the torment of savage brooding.

But he had never hated any one so much as that old man who turned up one evening to save him from an utter disaster, – from the conspiracy of the wretched sailors. He seemed to have fallen on board from the sky. His footsteps echoed on the empty steamer, and the strange deep-toned voice on deck repeating interrogatively the words, 'Mr Massy, Mr Massy there?' had been startling like a wonder. And coming up from the depths of the cold engine-room, where he had been pottering dismally with a candle amongst the enormous shadows, thrown on all sides by the skeleton limbs of machinery, Massy had been struck dumb by astonishment in the presence of that imposing old man with a beard like a silver plate, towering in the dusk rendered lurid by the expiring flames of sunset.

'Want to see me on business? What business? I am doing no business. Can't you see that this ship is laid up?' Massy had turned at bay before the pursuing irony of his disaster. Afterwards he could not believe his ears. What was that old fellow getting at? Things don't happen that way. It was a dream. He would presently wake up and find the man vanished like a shape of mist. The gravity, the dignity, the firm and courteous tone of that athletic old stranger impressed Massy. He was almost afraid. But it was no dream. Five hundreds pounds are no dream. At once he became suspicious. What did it mean? Of course it was an offer to catch hold of for dear life. But what could there be behind?

Before they had parted, after appointing a meeting in a solicitor's office early on the morrow, Massy was asking himself, What is his motive? He spent the night in hammering out the clauses of the agreement – a unique instrument of its sort whose tenor got bruited abroad somehow and became the talk and wonder of the port.

Massy's object had been to secure for himself as many ways as possible of getting rid of his partner without being called upon at once to pay back his share. Captain Whalley's efforts were directed to making the money secure. Was it not Ivy's money — a part of her fortune whose only other asset was the time-defying body of her old father? Sure of his forbearance in the strength of his love for her, he accepted, with stately serenity, Massy's stupidly cunning paragraphs against his incompetence, his dishonesty, his drunkenness, for the sake of other stringent stipulations. At the end of three years he was at liberty to withdraw from the partnership, taking his money with him. Provision was made for forming a fund to pay him off. But if he left the *Sofala* before the term, from whatever cause (barring death), Massy was to have a whole year for paying. 'Illness?' the lawyer had suggested: a young man fresh from Europe and not overburdened with business, who was rather amused. Massy began to whine unctuously, 'How could he be expected? . . .'

'Let that go,' Captain Whalley had said with a superb confidence in his body. 'Acts of God,' he added. In the midst of life we are in death, but he trusted his Maker with a still greater fearlessness — his Maker who knew his thoughts, his human affections, and his motives. His Creator knew what use he was making of his health — how much he wanted it . . . 'I trust my first illness will be my last. I've never been ill that I can remember,' he had remarked. 'Let it go.'

But at this early stage he had already awakened Massy's hostility by refusing to make it six hundred instead of five. 'I cannot do that,' was all he had said, simply, but with so much decision that Massy desisted at once from pressing the point, but had thought to himself, 'Can't! Old curmudgeon. *Won't!* He must have lots of money, but he would like to get hold of a soft berth and a sixth part of my profits for nothing if he only could.'

And during these years Massy's dislike grew under the restraint of something resembling fear. The simplicity of that man appeared dangerous. Of late he had changed, however, had appeared less formidable and with a lessened vigour of life, as though he had received a secret wound. But still he remained incomprehensible in his simplicity, fearlessness, and rectitude. And when Massy learned that he meant to leave him at the end of the time, to leave him confronted with the problem of the boilers, his dislike blazed up secretly into hate.

It had made him so clear-eyed that for a long time now Mr Sterne could have told him nothing he did not know. He had much ado in trying to terrorize that mean sneak into silence; he wanted to deal alone with the situation; and – incredible as it might have appeared to Mr Sterne – he had not yet given up the desire and the hope of inducing that hated old man to stay. Why! There was nothing else to do, unless he were to abandon his chances of fortune. But now, suddenly, since the crossing of the bar at Batu Beru things seemed to be coming rapidly to a point. It disquieted him so much that the study of the winning numbers failed to soothe his agitation: and the twilight in the cabin deepened, very sombre.

He put the list away, muttering once more, 'Oh, no, my boy, you don't. Not if I know it.' He did not mean the blinking, eavesdropping humbug to force his action. He took his head again into his hands; his immobility confined in the darkness of this shut-up little place seemed to make him a thing apart infinitely removed from the stir and the sounds of the deck.

He heard them: the passengers were beginning to jabber excitedly; somebody dragged a heavy box past his door. He heard Captain Whalley's voice above –

'Stations, Mr Sterne.' And the answer from somewhere on deck forward –

'Ay, ay, sir.'

'We shall moor head upstream this time; the ebb has made.'

'Head upstream, sir.'

'You will see to it, Mr Sterne.'

The answer was covered by the autocratic clang of the engine-room gong. The propeller went on beating slowly: one, two, three; one, two three – with pauses as if hesitating on the turn. The gong clanged time after time, and the water churned this way and that by the blades was making a great noisy commotion alongside. Mr Massy did not move. A shore-light on the other bank, a quarter of a mile across the river, drifted, no bigger than a tiny star, passing slowly athwart the circle of the port. Voices from Mr Van Wyk's jetty answered the hails from the ship; ropes were thrown and missed and thrown again; the swaying flame of a torch carried in a large sampan coming to fetch away in state the Rajah from down the coast cast a sudden ruddy glare into his cabin, over his very person. Mr Massy did not move. After a few last ponderous turns the engines stopped, and the prolonged clanging of the gong signified that the captain had done with them. A great number of boats and canoes of all sizes boarded the off-side of the *Sofala*. Then after a time the tumult of splashing, of cries, of shuffling feet, of packages dropped with a thump, the noise of the native passengers going away, subsided slowly. On the shore, a voice, cultivated, slightly authoritative, spoke very close alongside –

'Brought any mail for me this time?'

'Yes, Mr Van Wyk.' This was from Sterne, answering over the rail in a tone of respectful cordiality. 'Shall I bring it up to you?'

But the voice asked again –

'Where's the captain?'

'Still on the bridge, I believe. He hasn't left his chair. Shall I ...'

The voice interrupted negligently –

'I will come on board.'

'Mr Van Wyk.' Sterne suddenly broke out with an eager effort, 'will you do me the favour ...'

The mate walked away quickly towards the gangway. A silence fell. Mr Massy in the dark did not move.

He did not move even when he heard slow shuffling footsteps pass his cabin lazily. He contented himself to bellow out through the closed door –

'You – Jack !'

The footsteps came back without haste; the door-handle rattled, and the second engineer appeared in the opening, shadowy in the sheen of the skylight at his back, with his face apparently as black as the rest of his figure.

'We have been very long coming up this time,' Mr Massy growled, without changing his attitude.

'What do you expect with half the boiler tubes plugged up for leaks.' The second defended himself loquaciously.

'None of your lip,' said Massy.

'None of your rotten boilers — I say,' retorted his faithful subordinate without animation, huskily.

'Go down there and carry a head of steam on them yourself — if you dare. I don't.'

'You aren't worth your salt then,' Massy said. The other made a faint noise which resembled a laugh but might have been a snarl.

'Better go slow than stop the ship altogether,' he admonished his admired superior. Mr Massy moved at last. He turned in his chair, and grinding his teeth —

'Dam' you and the ship! I wish she were at the bottom of the sea. Then you would have to starve.'

The trusty second engineer closed the door gently.

Massy listened. Instead of passing on to the bathroom where he should have gone to clean himself, the second entered his cabin, which was next door. Mr Massy jumped up and waited. Suddenly he heard the lock snap in there. He rushed out and gave a violent kick to the door.

'I believe you are locking yourself up to get drunk,' he shouted.

A muffled answer came after a while.

'My own time.'

'If you take to boozing on the trip I'll fire you out,' Massy cried.

An obstinate silence followed that threat. Massy moved away, perplexed. On the bank two figures appeared, approaching the gangway. He heard a voice tinged with contempt —

'I would rather doubt your word. But I shall certainly speak to him of this.'

The other voice, Sterne's, said with a sort of regretful formality —

'Thanks. That's all I want. I must do my duty.'

Mr Massy was surprised. A short, dapper figure leaped lightly on the deck and nearly bounded into him where he stood beyond the circle of light from the gangway lamp. When it had passed towards the bridge, after exchanging a hurried 'Good evening', Massy said surlily to Sterne, who followed with slow steps —

'What is it you're making up to Mr Van Wyk for, now?'

'Far from it, Mr Massy. I am not good enough for Mr Van Wyk. Neither are you, sir, in his opinion, I am afraid. Captain Whalley is, it seems. He's gone to ask him to dine up at the house this evening.'

Then he murmured to himself darkly –

'I hope he will like it.'

12

MR Van Wyk, the white man of Batu Beru, an ex-naval officer who, for reasons best known to himself, had thrown away the promise of a brilliant career to become the pioneer of tobacco-planting on that remote part of the coast, had learned to like Captain Whalley. The appearance of the new skipper had attracted his attention. Nothing more unlike all the diverse types he had seen succeeding each other on the bridge of the *Sofala* could be imagined.

At that time Batu Beru was not what it has become since: the centre of a prosperous tobacco-growing district, a tropically suburban-looking little settlement of bungalows in one long street shaded with two rows of trees, embowered by the flowering and trim luxuriance of the gardens, with a three-mile-long carriage-road for the afternoon drives and a first-class Resident with a fat, cheery wife to lead the society of married estate-managers and unmarried young fellows in the service of the big companies.

All this prosperity was not yet; and Mr Van Wyk prospered alone on the left bank on his deep clearing carved out of the forest, which came down above and below to the water's edge. His lonely bungalow faced across the river the houses of the Sultan: a restless and melancholy old ruler who had done with love and war, for whom life no longer held any savour (except of evil forebodings) and time never had any value. He was afraid of death, and hoped he would die before the white men were ready to take his country from him. He crossed the river frequently (with never less than ten boats crammed full of people), in the wistful hope of extracting some information on

the subject from his own white man. There was a certain chair
on the verandah he always took: the dignitaries of the court
squatted on the rugs and skins between the furniture: the inferior people remained below on the grass-plot between the
house and the river in rows three or four deep all along the
front. Not seldom the visit began at daybreak. Mr Van Wyk
tolerated these inroads. He would nod out of his bedroom window, toothbrush or razor in hand, or pass through the throng of
courtiers in his bathing robe. He appeared and disappeared
humming a tune, polished his nails with attention, rubbed his
shaved face with eau-de-Cologne, drank his early tea, went out
to see his coolies at work; returned, looked through some papers
on his desk, read a page or two in a book or sat before his cottage
piano leaning back on the stool, his arms extended, fingers on the
keys, his body swaying slightly from side to side. When absolutely forced to speak he gave evasive, vaguely soothing answers
out of pure compassion: the same feeling perhaps made him so
lavishly hospitable with the aerated drinks that more than once
he left himself without soda-water for a whole week. That old
man had granted him as much land as he cared to have cleared:
it was neither more nor less than a fortune.

Whether it was fortune or seclusion from his kind that Mr
Van Wyk sought, he could not have pitched upon a better place.
Even the mail-boats of the subsidized company calling on the
veriest clusters of palm-thatched hovels along the coast steamed
past the mouth of Batu Beru river far away in the offing. The
contract was old: perhaps in a few years' time, when it had
expired, Batu Beru would be included in the service; meantime
all Mr Van Wyk's mail was addressed to Malacca, whence his
agent sent it across once a month by the *Sofala*. It followed that
whenever Massy had run short of money (through taking too
many lottery tickets), or got into a difficulty about a skipper,
Mr Van Wyk was deprived of his letters and newspapers. In so
far he had a personal interest in the fortunes of the *Sofala*.
Though he considered himself a hermit (and for no passing
whim evidently, since he had stood eight years of it already), he
liked to know what went on in the world.

Handy on the verandah upon a walnut *étagère* (it had come
last year by the *Sofala* – everything came by the *Sofala*) there lay,

piled up under bronze weights, a pile of *The Times* weekly
edition, the large sheets of the *Rotterdam Courant*, the *Graphic*
in its world-wide green wrappers, an illustrated Dutch publica-
tion without a cover, the numbers of a German magazine with
covers of the 'Bismarck malade' colour. There were also parcels
of new music – though the piano (it had come years ago by the
Sofala) in the damp atmosphere of the forests was generally out
of tune. It was vexing to be cut off from everything for sixty
days at a stretch sometimes, without any means of knowing
what was the matter. And when the *Sofala* reappeared Mr Van
Wyk would descend the steps of the verandah and stroll over the
grass-plot in front of his house, down to the water-side, with a
frown on his white brow.

'You've been laid up after an accident, I presume.'

He addressed the bridge, but before anybody could answer
Massy was sure to have already scrambled ashore over the rail
and pushed in, squeezing the palms of his hands together, bowing his sleek head as if gummed all over the top with black
threads and tapes. And he would be so enraged at the necessity of
having to offer such an explanation that his moaning would be
positively pitiful, while all the time he tried to compose his big
lips into a smile.

'No, Mr Van Wyk. You would not believe it. I couldn't get
one of those wretches to take the ship out. Not a single one of the
lazy beasts could be induced, and the law, you know, Mr Van
Wyk . . .'

He moaned at great length apologetically; the words conspiracy, plot, envy, came out prominently, whined with greater
energy. Mr Van Wyk, examining with a faint grimace his
polished fingernails, would say, 'H'm. Very unfortunate,' and
turn his back on him.

Fastidious, clever, slightly sceptical, accustomed to the best
society (he had held a much-envied shore appointment at the
Ministry of Marine for a year preceding his retreat from his pro-
fession and from Europe), he possessed a latent warmth of feeling and a capacity for sympathy which were concealed by a sort
of haughty, arbitrary indifference of manner arising from his
early training; and by a something an enemy might have called
foppish, in his aspect – like a distorted echo of past elegancies.

127

He managed to keep an almost military discipline amongst the coolies of the estate he had dragged into the light of day out of the tangle and shadows of the jungle; and the white shirt he put on every evening with its stiff glossy front and high collar looked as if he had meant to preserve the decent ceremony of evening-dress, but had wound a thick crimson sash above his hips as a concession to the wilderness, once his adversary, now his vanquished companion. Moreover, it was a hygienic precaution. Worn wide open in front, a short jacket of some airy silken stuff floated from his shoulders. His fluffy, fair hair, thin at the top, curled slightly at the sides; a carefully arranged moustache, an ungarnished forehead, the gleam of low patent shoes peeping under the wide bottom of trousers cut straight from the same stuff as the gossamer coat, completed a figure recalling, with its sash, a pirate chief of romance, and at the same time the elegance of a slightly bald dandy indulging, in seclusion, a taste for unorthodox costume.

It was his evening get-up. The proper time for the *Sofala* to arrive at Batu Beru was an hour before sunset, and he looked picturesque, and somehow quite correct, too, walking at the water's edge on the background of grass slope crowned with a low, long bungalow with an immensely steep roof of palm thatch, and clad to the eaves in flowering creepers. While the *Sofala* was being made fast he strolled in the shade of the few trees left near the landing-place, waiting till he could go on board. Her white men were not of his kind. The old Sultan (though his wistful invasions were a nuisance) was really much more acceptable to his fastidious taste. But still they were white; the periodical visits of the ship made a break in the well-filled sameness of the day without disturbing his privacy. Moreover, they were necessary from a business point of view; and through a strain of preciseness in his nature he was irritated when she failed to appear at the appointed time.

The cause of the irregularity was too absurd, and Massy, in his opinion, was a contemptible idiot. The first time the *Sofala* reappeared under the new agreement swinging out of the bend below, after he had almost given up all hope of ever seeing her again, he felt so angry that he did not go down at once to the landing-place. His servants had come running to him with the news, and he had dragged a chair close against the front rail of the verandah, spread his elbows out, rested his chin on his hands, and went on glaring at her fixedly while she was being made fast opposite his house. He could make out easily all the white faces on board. Who on earth was that kind of patriarch they had got there on the bridge now?

At last he sprang up and walked down the gravel path. It was a fact that the very gravel for his paths had been imported by the *Sofala*. Exasperated out of his quiet superciliousness, without looking at any one right or left, he accosted Massy straightway in so determined a manner that the engineer, taken aback, began to stammer unintelligibly. Nothing could be heard but the words: 'Mr Van Wyk ... Indeed, Mr Van Wyk ... For the future, Mr Van Wyk' – and by the suffusion of blood Massy's vast bilious face acquired an unnatural orange tint, out of which the disconcerted coal-black eyes shone in an extraordinary manner.

'Nonsense. I am tired of this. I wonder you have the impudence to come alongside my jetty as if I had it made for your convenience alone.'

Massy tried to protest earnestly. Mr Van Wyk was very angry. He had a good mind to ask that German firm – those people in Malacca – what was their name? – boats with green funnels. They would be only too glad of the opening to put one of their small steamers on the run. Yes; Schnitzler, Jacob Schnitzler, would in a moment. Yes. He had decided to write without delay.

In his agitation Massy caught up his falling pipe.

'You don't mean it, sir!' he shrieked.

'You shouldn't mismanage your business in this ridiculous manner.'

Mr Van Wyk turned on his heel. The other three whites on the bridge had not stirred during the scene. Massy walked hastily from side to side, puffed out his cheeks, suffocated.

'Stuck-up Dutchman!'

And he moaned out feverishly a long tale of griefs. The efforts he had made for all these years to please that man. This was the return you got for it, heh? Pretty. Write to Schnitzler – let in the green-funnel boats – get an old Hamburg Jew to ruin him. No, really he could laugh ... He laughed sobbingly ... Ha! ha! ha! And make him carry the letter in his own ship presumably.

He stumbled across a grating and swore. He would not hesitate to fling the Dutchman's correspondence overboard – the whole confounded bundle. He had never, never made any charge for that accommodation. But Captain Whalley, his new partner, would not let him probably; besides, it would be only putting off the evil day. For his own part he would make a hole in the water rather than look on tamely at the green funnels overrunning his trade.

He raved aloud. The China boys hung back with the dishes at the foot of the ladder. He yelled from the bridge down at the deck, 'Aren't we going to have any chow this evening at all?' then turned violently to Captain Whalley, who waited, grave and patient, at the head of the table, smoothing his beard in silence now and then with a forbearing gesture.

'You don't seem to care what happens to me. Don't you see that this affects your interests as much as mine? It's no joking matter.'

He took the foot of the table growling between his teeth.

'Unless you have a few thousands put away somewhere. I haven't.'

Mr Van Wyk dined in his thoroughly lit-up bungalow, putting a point of splendour in the night of his clearing above the dark bank of the river. Afterwards he sat down to his piano, and in a pause he became aware of slow footsteps passing on the path along the front. A plank or two creaked under a heavy tread; he swung half round on the music-stool, listening with his finger-tips at rest on the keyboard. His little terrier barked violently, backing in from the verandah. A deep voice apologized gravely for 'this intrusion'. He walked out quickly.

At the head of the steps the patriarchal figure, who was the new captain of the *Sofala* apparently (he had seen a round dozen of them, but not one of that sort), towered without advancing. The little dog barked unceasingly, till a flick of Mr Van Wyk's handkerchief made him spring aside into silence. Captain Whalley, opening the matter, was met by a punctiliously polite but determined opposition.

They carried on their discussion standing where they had come face to face. Mr Van Wyk observed his visitor with attention. Then at last, as if forced out of his reserve –

'I am surprised that you should intercede for such a confounded fool.'

This outbreak was almost complimentary, as if its meaning had been, 'That such a man as you should intercede!' Captain Whalley let it pass by without flinching. One would have thought he had heard nothing. He simply went on to state that he was personally interested in putting things straight between them. Personally . . .

But Mr Van Wyk, really carried away by his disgust with Massy, became very incisive –

'Indeed – if I am to be frank with you – his whole character does not seem to me particularly estimable or trustworthy . . .'

Captain Whalley, always straight, seemed to grow an inch taller and broader, as if the girth of his chest had suddenly expanded under his beard.

'My dear sir, you don't think I came here to discuss a man with whom I am – I am – h'm – closely associated.'

A sort of solemn silence lasted for a moment. He was not used to asking favours, but the importance he attached to this affair had made him willing to try . . . Mr Van Wyk, favourably impressed, and suddenly mollified by a desire to laugh, interrupted –

'That's all right if you make it a personal matter; but you can do no less than sit down and smoke a cigar with me.'

A slight pause, then Captain Whalley stepped forward heavily. As to the regularity of the service, for the future he made himself responsible for it; and his name was Whalley – perhaps to a sailor (he was speaking to a sailor, was he not?) not altogether unfamiliar. There was a lighthouse now, on an island. Maybe Mr Van Wyk himself . . .

'Oh, yes. Oh, indeed.' Mr Van Wyk caught on at once. He indicated a chair. How very interesting. For his own part he had seen some service in the last Acheen War, but had never been so far East. Whalley Island? Of course. Now that was very interesting. What changes his guest must have seen since.

'I can look further back even – on a whole half-century.'

Captain Whalley expanded a bit. The flavour of a good cigar (it was a weakness) had gone straight to his heart, also the civility of that young man. There was something in that accidental contact of which he had been starved in his years of struggle.

The front wall retreating made a square recess furnished like a room. A lamp with a milky glass shade, suspended below the slope of the high roof at the end of a slender brass chain, threw a bright round of light upon a little table bearing an open book and an ivory paper-knife. And, in the translucent shadows beyond, other tables could be seen, a number of easy-chairs of various shapes with a great profusion of skin rugs strewn on the teakwood planking all over the verandah. The flowering creepers scented the air. Their foliage clipped out between the uprights made as if several frames of thick, unstirring leaves reflecting the lamplight in a green glow. Through the opening at his elbow Captain Whalley could see the gangway lantern of the *Sofala* burning dim by the shore, the shadowy masses of the town beyond the open lustrous darkness of the river, and, as if hung along the straight edge of the projecting eaves, a narrow black strip of the night sky full of stars – resplendent. The famous cigar in hand he had a moment of complacency.

'A trifle. Somebody must lead the way. I just showed that the thing could be done; but you men brought up to the use of steam cannot conceive the vast importance of my bit of venturesomeness to the Eastern trade of the time. Why, that new route reduced the average time of a southern passage by eleven days for more than half the year. Eleven days! It's on record. But the remarkable thing – speaking to a sailor – I should say was ...'

He talked well, without egotism, professionally. The powerful voice, produced without effort, filled the bungalow even into the empty rooms with a deep and limpid resonance, seemed to make a stillness outside; and Mr Van Wyk was surprised by the serene quality of its tone, like the perfection of manly gentleness. Nursing one small foot, in a silk sock and a patent leather shoe, on his knee, he was immensely entertained. It was as if nobody could talk like this now, and the over-shadowed eyes, the flowing white beard, the big frame, the serenity, the whole temper of the man, were an amazing survival from the prehistoric times of the world coming up to him out of the sea.

Captain Whalley had been also the pioneer of the early trade in the Gulf of Pe-tchi-li. He even found occasion to mention that he had buried his 'dear wife' there six-and-twenty years ago. Mr Van Wyk, impassive, could not help speculating in his mind swiftly as to the sort of woman that would mate with such a man. Did they make an adventurous and well-matched pair? No. Very possibly she had been small, frail, no doubt very feminine – or most likely commonplace with domestic instincts, utterly insignificant. But Captain Whalley was no garrulous bore, and shaking his head as if to dissipate the momentary gloom that had settled on his handsome old face, he alluded conversationally to Mr Van Wyk's solitude.

Mr Van Wyk affirmed that sometimes he had more company than he wanted. He mentioned smilingly some of the peculiarities of his intercourse with 'My Sultan'. He made his visits in force. Those people damaged his grass-plot in front (it was not easy to obtain some approach to a lawn in the tropics), and the other day had broken down some rare bushes he had planted over there. And Captain Whalley remembered immediately that, in 'forty-seven, the then Sultan, 'this man's grandfather', had been notorious as a great protector of the piratical fleets of praus from farther East. They had a safe refuge in the river at Batu Beru. He financed more especially a Balinini chief called Haji Daman. Captain Whalley, nodding significantly his bushy white eyebrows, had very good reason to know something of that. The world had progressed since that time.

Mr Van Wyk demurred with unexpected acrimony. Progressed in what? he wanted to know.

Why, in knowledge of truth, in decency, in justice, in order – in honesty, too, since men harmed each other mostly from ignorance. It was, Captain Whalley concluded quaintly, more pleasant to live in.

Mr Van Wyk whimsically would not admit that Mr Massy, for instance, was more pleasant naturally than the Balinini pirates.

The river had not gained much by the change. They were in their way every bit as honest. Massy was less ferocious than Haji Daman no doubt, but . . .

'And what about you, my good sir?' Captain Whalley laughed a deep soft laugh. '*You* are an improvement, surely.'

He continued in a vein of pleasantry. A good cigar was better than a knock on the head – the sort of welcome he would have found on this river forty or fifty years ago. Then leaning forward slightly, he became earnestly serious. It seems as if, outside their own sea-gipsy tribes, these rovers had hated all mankind with an incomprehensible, bloodthirsty hatred. Meantime their depredations had been stopped, and what was the consequence? The new generation was orderly, peaceable, settled in prosperous villages. He could speak from personal knowledge. And even the few survivors of that time – old men now – had changed so much, that it would have been unkind to remember against them that they had ever slit a throat in their lives. He had one especially in his mind's eye: a dignified, venerable headman of a certain large coast village about sixty miles sou'west of Tampasuk. It did one's heart good to see him – to hear that man speak. He might have been a ferocious savage once. What men wanted was to be checked by superior intelligence, by superior knowledge, by superior force, too – yes, by force held in trust from God and sanctified by its use in accordance with His declared will. Captain Whalley believed a disposition for good existed in every man, even if the world were not a very happy place as a whole. In the wisdom of men he had not so much confidence.

The disposition had to be helped up pretty sharply sometimes, he admitted. They might be silly, wrong-headed, unhappy; but naturally evil – no. There was at bottom a complete harmlessness at least . . .

'Is there?' Mr Van Wyk snapped acrimoniously.

Captain Whalley laughed at the interjection, in the good humour of large, tolerating certitude. He could look back at half a century, he pointed out. The smoke oozed placidly through the white hairs hiding his kindly lips.

'At all events,' he resumed after a pause, 'I am glad that they've had no time to do you much harm as yet.'

This allusion to his comparative youthfulness did not offend Mr Van Wyk, who got up and wriggled his shoulders with an enigmatic half-smile. They walked out together amicably into the starry night towards the river-side. Their footsteps resounded unequally on the dark path. At the shore end of the gangway the lantern, hung low to the handrail, threw a vivid light on the white legs and the big black feet of Mr Massy waiting about anxiously. From the waist upwards he remained shadowy, with a row of buttons gleaming up to the vague outline of his chin.

'You may thank Captain Whalley for this,' Mr Van Wyk said, curtly, to him before turning away.

The lamps on the verandah flung three long squares of light between the uprights far over the grass. A bat flitted before his face like a circling flake of velvety blackness. Along the jasmine hedge the night air seemed heavy with the fall of perfumed dew; flowerbeds bordered the path; the clipped bushes uprose in dark, rounded clumps here and there before the house; the dense foliage of creepers filtered the sheen of the lamplight within in a soft glow all along the front; and everything near and far stood still in a great immobility, in a great sweetness.

Mr Van Wyk (a few years before he had had occasion to imagine himself treated more badly than anybody alive had ever been by a woman) felt for Captain Whalley's optimistic views the disdain of a man who had once been credulous himself. His disgust with the world (the woman for a time had filled it for him completely) had taken the form of activity in retirement, because, though capable of great depth of feeling, he was energetic and essentially practical. But there was in that uncommon old sailor, drifting on the outskirts of his busy solitude, something that fascinated his scepticism. His very simplicity (amusing enough) was like a delicate refinement of an upright character. The striking dignity of manner could be nothing else, in a man reduced to such a humble position, but the expression of something essentially noble in the character. With all his trust in mankind he was no fool; the serenity of his temper at the end of so many years, since it could not obviously have been appeased by success, wore an air of profound wisdom. Mr Van Wyk was amused at it sometimes. Even the very physical traits of the old captain of the *Sofala*, his powerful frame, his reposeful mien, his intelligent, handsome face, the big limbs, the benign courtesy, the touch of rugged severity in the shaggy eyebrows, made up a seductive personality. Mr Van Wyk disliked littleness of every kind, but there was nothing small about that man, and in the exemplary regularity of many trips an intimacy had grown up between them, a warm feeling at bottom under a kindly stateliness of forms agreeable to his fastidiousness.

They kept their respective opinions on all worldly matters. His other convictions Captain Whalley never intruded. The difference of their ages was like another bond between them. Once, when twitted with the uncharitableness of his youth, Mr Van Wyk, running his eye over the vast proportions of his interlocutor, retorted in friendly banter –

'Oh. You'll come to my way of thinking yet. You'll have plenty of time. Don't call yourself old: you look good for a round hundred.'

But he could not help his stinging incisiveness, and though moderating it by an almost affectionate smile, he added –

'And by then you will probably consent to die from sheer disgust.'

Captain Whalley, smiling, too, shook his head. 'God forbid!'

He thought that perhaps on the whole he deserved something better than to die in such sentiments. The time of course would have to come, and he trusted to his Maker to provide a manner of going out of which he need not be ashamed. For the rest he hoped he would live to a hundred if need be; other men had been known; it would be no miracle. He expected no miracles.

The pronounced, argumentative tone caused Mr Van Wyk to raise his head and look at him steadily. Captain Whalley was gazing fixedly with a rapt expression, as though he had seen his Creator's favourable decree written in mysterious characters on the wall. He kept perfectly motionless for a few seconds, then got his vast bulk on to his feet so impetuously that Mr Van Wyk was startled.

He struck first a heavy blow on his inflated chest: and, throwing out horizontally a big arm that remained steady, extended in the air like the limb of a tree on a windless day –

'Not a pain or an ache there. Can you see this shake in the least?'

His voice was low, in an awing, confident contrast with the headlong emphasis of his movements. He sat down abruptly.

'This isn't to boast of it, you know. I am nothing,' he said in his effortless strong voice, that seemed to come out as naturally as a river flows. He picked up the stump of the cigar he had laid aside, and added peacefully, with a slight nod, 'As it happens, my life is necessary; it isn't my own, it isn't – God knows.'

He did not say much for the rest of the evening, but several times Mr Van Wyk detected a faint smile of assurance flitting under the heavy moustache.

Later on Captain Whalley would now and then consent to dine 'at the house'. He could even be induced to drink a glass of wine. 'Don't think I'm afraid of it, my good sir,' he explained. 'There was a very good reason why I should give it up.'

On another occasion, leaning back at ease, he remarked, 'You have treated me most – most humanely, my dear Mr Van Wyk, from the very first.'

'You'll admit there was some merit,' Mr Van Wyk hinted, slily. 'An associate of that excellent Massy ... Well, well, my dear captain, I won't say a word against him.'

'It would be no use your saying anything against him,' Captain Whalley affirmed a little moodily. 'As I've told you before, my life – my work, is necessary, not for myself alone. I can't choose ...' He paused, turned the glass before him right round ... 'I have an only child – a daughter.'

The ample downward sweep of his arm over the table seemed to suggest a small girl at a vast distance. 'I hope to see her once more before I die. Meantime it's enough to know that she has me sound and solid, thank God. You can't understand how one feels. Bone of my bone, flesh of my flesh; the very image of my poor wife. Well, she ...'

Again he paused, then pronounced stoically the words, 'She has a hard struggle.'

And his head fell on his breast, his eyebrows remained knitted, as by an effort of meditation. But generally his mind seemed steeped in the serenity of boundless trust in a higher power. Mr Van Wyk wondered sometimes how much of it was due to the splendid vitality of the man, to the bodily vigour which seems to impart something of its force to the soul. But he had learned to like him very much.

13

THIS was the reason why Mr Sterne's confidential communication, delivered hurriedly on the shore alongside the dark silent ship, had disturbed his equanimity. It was the most incomprehensible and unexpected thing that could happen; and the perturbation of his spirit was so great that, forgetting all about his letters, he ran rapidly up the bridge ladder.

The portable table was being put together for dinner to the left of the wheel by two pig-tailed 'boys', who as usual snarled at each other over the job, while another, a doleful, burly, very yellow Chinaman, resembling Mr Massy, waited apathetically with the cloth over his arm and a pile of thick dinner-plates against his chest. A common cabin lamp with its globe missing, brought up from below, had been hooked to the wooden framework of the awning; the sidescreens had been lowered all round; Captain Whalley, filling the depths of the wicker-chair, seemed to sit benumbed in a canvas tent crudely lighted, and used for the storing of nautical objects; a shabby steering-wheel, a battered brass binnacle on a stout mahogany stand, two dingy lifebuoys, an old cork fender lying in a corner, dilapidated decklockers with loops of tin rope instead of door-handles.

He shook off the appearance of numbness to return Mr Van Wyk's unusually brisk greeting, but relapsed directly afterwards. To accept a pressing invitation to dinner 'up at the house' cost him another very visible physical effort. Mr Van Wyk, perplexed, folded his arms, and leaning back against the rail, with his little, black, shiny feet well out, examined him covertly.

'I've noticed of late that you are not quite yourself, old friend.'

He put an affectionate gentleness into the last two words. The real intimacy of their intercourse had never been so vividly expressed before.

'Tut, tut, tut!'

The wicker-chair creaked heavily.

'Irritable,' commented Mr Van Wyk to himself; and aloud, 'I'll expect to see you in half an hour, then,' he said, negligently, moving off.

'In half an hour,' Captain Whalley's rigid silvery head repeated behind him as if out of a trance.

Amidships, below, two voices, close against the engine-room, could be heard answering each other – one angry and slow, the other alert.

'I tell you the beast has locked himself in to get drunk.'

'Can't help it now, Mr Massy. After all, a man has a right to shut himself up in his cabin in his own time.'

'Not to get drunk.'

'I heard him swear that the worry with the boilers was enough to drive any man to drink,' Sterne said, maliciously.

Massy hissed out something about bursting the door in. Mr Van Wyk, to avoid them, crossed in the dark to the other side of the deserted deck. The planking of the little wharf rattled faintly under his hasty feet.

'Mr Van Wyk ! Mr Van Wyk !'

He walked on: somebody was running on the path. 'You've forgotten to get your mail.'

Sterne, holding a bundle of papers in his hand, caught up with him.

'Oh, thanks.'

But, as the other continued at his elbow, Mr Van Wyk stopped short. The overhanging eaves, descending low upon the lighted front of the bungalow, threw their black straight-edged shadow into the great body of the night on that side. Everything was very still. A tinkle of cutlery and a slight jingle of glasses were heard. Mr Van Wyk's servants were laying the table for two on the verandah.

'I am afraid you give me no credit whatever for my good intentions in the matter I've spoken to you about,' said Sterne.

'I simply don't understand you.'

'Captain Whalley is a very audacious man, but he will understand that his game is up. That's all that anybody need ever know of it from me. Believe me, I am very considerate in this, but duty is duty. I don't want to make a fuss. All I ask you, as his friend, is to tell him from me that the game's up. That will be sufficient.'

Mr Van Wyk felt a loathsome dismay at this queer privilege of friendship. He would not demean himself by asking for the slightest explanation; to drive the other away with contumely he did not think prudent – as yet, at any rate. So much assurance staggered him. Who could tell what there could be in it? he thought. His regard for Captain Whalley had the tenacity of a disinterested sentiment, and his practical instinct coming to his aid, he concealed his scorn.

'I gather, then, that this is something grave.'

'Very grave,' Sterne assented, solemnly, delighted at having produced an effect at last. He was ready to add some effusive protestations of regret at the 'unavoidable necessity', but Mr Van Wyk cut him short – very civilly, however.

Once on the verandah Mr Van Wyk put his hands in his pockets, and, straddling his legs, stared down at a black panther skin lying on the floor before a rocking-chair. 'It looks as if the fellow had not the pluck to play his own precious game openly,' he thought.

This was true enough. In the face of Massy's last rebuff Sterne dared not declare his knowledge. His object was simply to get charge of the steamer and keep it for some time. Massy would never forgive him for forcing himself on; but if Captain Whalley left the ship of his own accord, the command would devolve upon him for the rest of the trip; so he hit upon the brilliant idea of scaring the old man away. A vague menace, a mere hint, would be enough in such a brazen case; and, with a strange admixture of compassion, he thought that Batu Beru was a very good place for throwing up the sponge. The skipper could go ashore quietly, and stay with that Dutchman of his. Weren't these two as thick as thieves together? And on reflection he seemed to see that there was a way to work the whole thing through that great friend of the old man's. This was another brilliant idea. He had an inborn preference for circuitous methods. In this particular case he desired to remain in the background as much as possible, to avoid exasperating Massy needlessly. No fuss! Let it all happen naturally.

Mr Van Wyk all through the dinner was conscious of a sense of isolation that invades sometimes the closeness of human intercourse. Captain Whalley failed lamentably and obviously in his attempts to eat something. He seemed overcome by a strange absentmindedness. His hand would hover irresolutely, as if left without guidance by a preoccupied mind. Mr Van Wyk had heard him coming up from a long way off in the profound still-ness of the river-side, and had noticed the irresolute character of the footfalls. The toe of his boot had struck the bottom stair as though he had come along mooning with his head in the air right up to the steps of the verandah. Had the captain of the *Sofala* been another sort of man he would have suspected the work of age there. But one glance at him was enough. Time – after, indeed, marking him for its own – had given him up to his usefulness, in which his simple faith would see a proof of Divine mercy. 'How could I contrive to warn him?' Mr Van Wyk wondered, as if Captain Whalley had been miles and miles away, out of sight and earshot of all evil. He was sickened by an immense disgust of Sterne. To even mention his threat to a man like Whalley would be positively indecent. There was something more vile and insulting in its hint than in a definite charge of crime – the debasing taint of blackmailing. 'What could any one bring against him?' he asked himself. This was a limpid person-ality. 'And for what object?' The Power that man trusted had thought fit to leave him nothing on earth that envy could lay hold of, except a bare crust of bread.

'Won't you try some of this?' he asked, pushing a dish slightly. Suddenly it occurred to Mr Van Wyk that Sterne might possibly be coveting the command of the *Sofala*. His cynicism was quite startled by what looked like a proof that no man may count himself safe from his kind unless in the very abyss of misery. An intrigue of that sort was hardly worth troubling about, he judged; but still, with such a fool as Massy to deal with, Whalley ought to and must be warned.

At this moment Captain Whalley, bolt upright, the deep cavities of the eyes overhung by a bushy frown, and one large brown hand resting on each side of his empty plate, spoke across the table-cloth abruptly –

'Mr Van Wyk, you've always treated me with the most humane consideration.'

'My dear captain, you make too much of the simple fact that I am not a savage.' Mr Van Wyk, utterly revolted by the thought of Sterne's obscure attempt, raised his voice incisively, as if the mate had been hiding somewhere within earshot. 'Any consideration I have been able to show was no more than the rightful due of a character I've learned to regard by this time with an esteem that nothing can shake.'

A slight ring of glass made him lift his eyes from the slice of pineapple he was cutting into small pieces on his plate. In changing his position Captain Whalley had contrived to upset an empty tumbler.

Without looking that way, leaning sideways on his elbow, his other hand shading his brow, he groped shadily for it, then desisted. Van Wyk stared blankly, as if something momentous had happened all at once. He did not know why he should feel so startled; but he forgot Sterne utterly for the moment.

'Why, what's the matter?'

And Captain Whalley, half-averted, in a deadened, agitated voice, muttered –

'Esteem!'

'And I may add something more,' Mr Van Wyk, very steady-eyed, pronounced slowly.

'Hold! Enough!' Captain Whalley did not change his attitude or raise his voice. 'Say no more! I can make you no return. I am too poor even for that now. Your esteem is worth having. You are not a man that would stoop to deceive the poorest sort of devil on earth, or make a ship unseaworthy every time he takes her to sea.'

Mr Van Wyk, leaning forward, his face gone pink all over, with the starched table-napkin over his knees, was inclined to mistrust his senses, his power of comprehension, the sanity of his guest.

'Where? Why? In the name of God! – what's this? What ship? I don't understand who ...'

'Then, in the name of God, it is I! A ship's unseaworthy when her captain can't see. I am going blind.'

Mr Van Wyk made a slight movement, and sat very still afterwards for a few seconds; then, with the thought of Sterne's 'The game's up', he ducked under the table to pick up the napkin which had slipped off his knees. This was the game that was up. And at the same time the muffled voice of Captain Whalley passed over him –

'I've deceived them all. Nobody knows.'

He emerged flushed to the eyes. Captain Whalley, motionless under the full blaze of the lamp, shaded his face with his hand.

'And you had that courage?'

'Call it by what name you like. But you are a humane man – a – a – gentleman, Mr Van Wyk. You may have asked me what I had done with my conscience.'

He seemed to muse, profoundly silent, very still in his mournful pose.

'I began to tamper with it in my pride. You begin to see a lot of things when you are going blind. I could not be frank with an old chum even. I was not frank with Massy – no, not altogether. I knew he took me for a wealthy sailor fool, and I let him. I wanted to keep up my importance – because there was poor Ivy away there – my daughter. What did I want to trade on his misery for? I did trade on it – for her. And now, what mercy could I expect from him? He would trade on mine if he knew it. He would hunt the old fraud out, and stick to the money for a year. Ivy's money. And I haven't kept a penny for myself. How am I going to live for a year. A year! In a year there will be no sun in the sky for her father.'

His deep voice came out, awfully veiled, as though he had been overwhelmed by the earth of a landslide and talking of the thoughts that haunt the dead in their graves. A cold shudder ran down Mr Van Wyk's back.

'And how long is it since you have . . .?' he began.

'It was a long time before I could bring myself to believe in this – this – visitation.' Captain Whalley spoke with gloomy patience from under his hand.

He had not thought he had deserved it. He had begun by deceiving himself from day to day, from week to week. He had the Serang at hand there – an old servant. It came on gradually, and when he could no longer deceive himself . . .

His voice died out almost.

'Rather than give her up I set myself to deceive you all.'

'It's incredible,' whispered Mr Van Wyk. Captain Whalley's appalling murmur flowed on.

'Not even the sign of God's anger could make me forget her. How could I forsake my child, feeling my vigour all the time – the blood warm within me? Warm as yours. It seems to me that, like the blinded Samson, I would find the strength to shake down a temple upon my head. She's a struggling woman – my own child that we used to pray over together, my poor wife and I. Do you remember that day I as well as told you that I believed God would let me live to a hundred for her sake? What sin is there in loving your child? Do you see it? I was ready for her sake to live for ever. I half believed I would. I've been praying for death since. Ha! Presumptuous man – you wanted to live . . .'

A tremendous, shuddering upheaval of that big frame, shaken by a gasping sob, set the glasses jingling all over the table, seemed to make the whole house tremble to the roof-tree. And Mr Van Wyk, whose feeling of outraged love had been translated into a form of struggle with nature, understood very well that, for that man whose whole life had been conditioned by action, there could exist no other expression for all the emotions; that, to voluntarily cease venturing, doing, enduring, for his child's sake, would have been exactly like plucking his warm love for her out of his living heart. Something too monstrous, too impossible, even to conceive.

Captain Whalley had not changed his attitude, that seemed to express something of shame, sorrow, and defiance.

'I have even deceived you. If it had not been for that word "esteem". These are not the words for me. I would have lied to you. Haven't I lied to you? Weren't you going to trust your property on board this very trip?'

'I have a floating yearly policy,' Mr Van Wyk said almost unwittingly, and was amazed at the sudden cooping up of a commercial detail.

'The ship is unseaworthy, I tell you. The policy would be invalid if it were known . . .'

'We shall share the guilt, then.'

'Nothing could make mine less,' said Captain Whalley.

He had not dared to consult a doctor; the man would have perhaps asked who he was, what he was doing; Massy might have heard something. He had lived on without any help, human or divine. The very prayers stuck in his throat. What was there to pray for? and death seemed as far as ever. Once he got into his cabin he dared not come out again; when he sat down he dared not get up; he dared not raise his eyes to anybody's face, he felt reluctant to look upon the sea or up to the sky. The world was fading before his great fear of giving himself away. The old ship was his last friend; he was not afraid of her; he knew every inch of her deck; but at her, too, he hardly dared to look, for fear of finding he could see less than the day before. A great incertitude enveloped him. The horizon was gone; the sky mingled darkly with the sea. Who was this figure standing over yonder? what was this thing lying down there? And a frightful doubt of the reality of what he could see made even the remnant of sight that remained to him an added torment, a pitfall always open for his miserable pretence. He was afraid to stumble inexcusably over something – to say a fatal Yes or No to a question. The hand of God was upon him, but it could not tear him away from his child. And, as if in a nightmare of humiliation, every featureless man seemed an enemy.

He let his hand fall heavily on the table. Mr Van Wyk, arms down, chin on breast, with a gleam of white teeth pressing on the lower lip, meditated on Sterne's 'The game's up'.

'The Serang of course does not know.'

'Nobody,' said Captain Whalley, with assurance.

'Ah, yes. Nobody. Very well. Can you keep it up to the end of the trip? That is the last under the agreement with Massy.'

Captain Whalley got up and stood erect, very stately, with the great white beard lying like a silver breastplate over the awful secret of his heart. Yes; that was the only hope there was for him of ever seeing her again, of securing the money, the last he could do for her, before he crept away somewhere – useless, a burden, a reproach to himself. His voice faltered.

'Think of it! Never see her any more: the only human being besides myself now on earth that can remember my wife. She's just like her mother. Lucky the poor woman is where there are no tears shed over those they loved on earth and that remain to pray not to be led into temptation – because, I suppose, the blessed know the secret of grace in God's dealings with His created children.'

He swayed a little, said with austere dignity –

'I don't. I know only the child He has given me.'

And he began to walk. Mr Van Wyk, jumping up, saw the full meaning of the rigid head, the hesitating feet, the vaguely extended hand. His heart was beating fast; he moved a chair aside, and instinctively advanced as if to offer his arm. But Captain Whalley passed him by, making for the stairs quite straight.

'He could not see me at all out of his line,' Van Wyk thought, with a sort of awe. Then going to the head of the stairs, he asked a little tremulously –

'What is it like – like a mist – like ...' Captain Whalley, half-way down, stopped, and turned round undismayed to answer:

'It is as if the light were ebbing out of the world. Have you ever watched the ebbing sea on an open stretch of sands withdrawing farther and farther away from you? It is like this – only there will be no flood to follow. Never. It is as if the sun were growing smaller, the stars going out one by one. There can't be many left that I can see by this. But I haven't had the courage to look of late ...' He must have been able to make out Mr Van Wyk, because he checked him by an authoritative gesture and a stoical –

'I can get about alone yet.'

It was as if he had taken his line, and would accept no help from men, after having been cast out, like a presumptuous Titan, from his heaven. Mr Van Wyk, arrested, seemed to count the footsteps right out of earshot. He walked between the tables, tapping smartly with his heels, took up a paper-knife, dropped it after a vague glance along the blade; then happening upon the piano, struck a few chords, standing up before the keyboard with an attentive poise of the head like a piano-tuner; closing it, he pivoted on his heels brusquely, avoided the little terrier sleeping trustfully on crossed forepaws, came upon the stairs next, and, as though he had lost his balance on the top step, ran down head-long out of the house. His servants, beginning to clear the table, heard him mutter to himself (evil words no doubt) down there, and then after a pause go away with a strolling gait in the direction of the wharf.

The bulwarks of the *Sofala* lying alongside the bank made a low, black wall on the undulating contour of the shore. Two masts and a funnel uprose from behind it with a great rake, as if about to fall: a solid, square elevation in the middle bore the ghostly shapes of white boats, the curves of davits, lines of rail and stanchions, all confused and mingling darkly everywhere;

but low down, amidships, a single lighted port stared out on the night, perfectly round, like a small, full moon, whose yellow beam caught a patch of wet mud, the edge of trodden grass, two turns of heavy cable wound round the foot of a thick wooden post in the ground.

Mr Van Wyk, peering alongside, heard a muzzy boastful voice apparently jeering at a person called Prendergast. It mouthed abuse thickly, choked; then pronounced very distinctly the word 'Murphy', and chuckled. Glass tinkled tremulously. All these sounds came from the lighted port. Mr Van Wyk hesitated, stooped; it was impossible to look through unless he went down into the mud.

'Sterne – of course. Look at him blink. Look at him! Sterne, Whalley, Massy. Massy, Whalley, Sterne. But Massy's the best. You can't come over him. He would just love to see you starve.'

Mr Van Wyk moved away, made out farther forward a shadowy head stuck out from under the awnings as if on the watch, and spoke quietly in Malay, 'Is the mate asleep?'

'No. Here, at your service.'

In a moment Sterne appeared, walking as noiselessly as a cat on the wharf.

'It's so jolly dark, and I had no idea you would be down to-night.'

'What's this horrible raving?' asked Mr Van Wyk, as if to explain the cause of a shudder that ran over him audibly.

'Jack's broken out on a drunk. That's our second. It's his way. He will be right enough by tomorrow afternoon, only Mr Massy will keep on worrying up and down the deck. We had better get away.'

He muttered suggestively of a talk 'up at the house'. He had long desired to effect an entrance there, but Mr Van Wyk nonchalantly demurred: it would not, he feared, be quite prudent, perhaps; and the opaque black shadow under one of the two big trees left at the landing-place swallowed them up, impenetrably dense by the side of the wide river, that seemed to spin into threads of glitter the light of a few big stars dropped here and there upon its outspread and flowing stillness.

'The situation is grave beyond doubt,' Mr Van Wyk said. Ghost-like in their white clothes they could not distinguish each other's features, and their feet made no sound on the soft earth. A sort of purring was heard. Mr Sterne felt gratified by such a beginning.

'I thought, Mr Van Wyk, a gentleman of your sort would see at once how awkwardly I was situated.'

'Yes, very. Obviously his health is bad. Perhaps he's breaking up. I see, and he himself is well aware – I assume I am speaking to a man of sense – he is well aware that his legs are giving out.'

'His legs – ah !' Mr Sterne was disconcerted, and then turned sulky. 'You may call it his legs if you like; what I want to know is whether he intends to clear out quietly. That's a good one, too ! His legs ! Pooh !'

'Why, yes. Only look at the way he walks,' Van Wyk took him up in a perfectly cool and undoubting tone. 'The question, however, is whether your sense of duty does not carry you too far from your true interest. After all, I, too, could do something to serve you. You know who I am.'

'Everybody along the Straits has heard of you, sir.'

Mr Van Wyk presumed that this meant something favourable. Sterne had a soft laugh at this pleasantry. He should think so ! To the opening statement, that the partnership agreement was to expire at the end of this very trip, he gave an attentive assent. He was aware. One heard of nothing else on board all the blessed day long. As to Massy, it was no secret that he was in a jolly deep hole with these worn-out boilers. He would have to borrow somewhere a couple of hundred first of all to pay off the captain; and then he would have to raise money on mortgage upon the ship for new boilers – that is, if he could find a lender at all. At best it meant loss of time, a break in the trade, short earnings for the year – and there was always the danger of having his connection filched away from him by the Germans. It was whispered about that he had already tried two firms. Neither would have anything to do with him. Ship too old, and the man too well known in the place . . . Mr Sterne's final rapid winking remained buried in the deep darkness sibilating with his whispers.

'Supposing, then, he got the loan,' Mr Van Wyk resumed in a deliberate undertone, 'on your own showing he's more than likely to get a mortgagee's man thrust upon him as captain. For my part, I know that I would make that very stipulation myself if I had to find the money. And as a matter of fact I am thinking of doing so. It would be worth my while in many ways. Do you see how this would bear on the case under discussion?'

'Thank you, sir. I am sure you couldn't get anybody that would care more for your interests.'

'Well, it suits my interest that Captain Whalley should finish his time. I shall probably take a passage with you down the Straits. If that can be done, I'll be on the spot when all these changes take place, and in a position to look after *your* interests.'

'Mr Van Wyk, I want nothing better. I am sure I am infinitely . . .'

'I take it, then, that this may be done without any trouble.'

'Well, sir, what risk there is can't be helped; but (speaking to you as my employer now) the thing is more safe than it looks. If anybody had told me of it I wouldn't have believed it, but I have been looking on myself. That old Serang has been trained up to the game. There's nothing the matter with his – his – limbs, sir. He's got used to do things on his own in a remarkable way. And let me tell you, sir, that Captain Whalley, poor man, is by no means useless. Fact. Let me explain to you, sir. He stiffens up that old monkey of a Malay, who knows well enough what to do. Why, he must have kept captain's watches in all sorts of country ships off and on for the last five-and-twenty years. These natives, sir, as long as they have a white man close at the back, will go on doing the right thing most surprisingly well – even if left quite to themselves. Only the white man must be of the sort to put starch into them, and the captain is just the one for that. Why, sir, he has drilled him so well that now he needs hardly speak at all. I have seen that little wrinkled ape made to take the ship out of Pangu Bay on a blowy morning and on all through the islands; take her out first-rate, sir, dodging under the old man's elbow, and in such quiet style that you could not have told for the life of you which of the two was doing the work up there. That's where our poor friend would be still of use to the ship even if – if – he could no longer lift a foot, sir. Providing the Serang does not know that there's anything wrong.'

'He doesn't.'

'Naturally not. Quite beyond his apprehension. They aren't capable of finding out anything about us, sir.'

'You seem to be a shrewd man,' said Mr Van Wyk in a choked mutter, as though he were feeling sick.

'You'll find me a good enough servant, sir.'

Mr Sterne hoped now for a handshake at least, but unexpectedly with a 'What's this? Better not to be seen together', Mr Van Wyk's white shape wavered, and instantly seemed to melt away in the black air under the roof of boughs. The mate was startled. Yes. There was that faint thumping clatter.

He stole out silently from under the shade. The lighted porthole shone from afar. His head swam with the intoxication of sudden success. What a thing it was to have a gentleman to deal with! He crept aboard, and there was something weird in the shadowy stretch of empty decks, echoing with shouts and blows proceeding from a darker part amidships. Mr Massy was raging before the door of the berth: the drunken voice within flowed on undisturbed in the violent racket of kicks.

'Shut up! Put your light out and turn in, you confounded swilling pig – you! D'you hear me, you beast?'

The kicking stopped, and in the pause the muzzy oracular voice announced from within –

'Ah! Massy, now – that's another thing. Massy's deep.'

'Who's that aft there? You, Sterne? He'll drink himself into a fit of horrors.' The chief engineer appeared vague and big at the corner of the engine-room skylight.

'He will be good enough for duty tomorrow. I would let him be, Mr Massy.'

Sterne slipped away into his berth, and at once had to sit down. His head swam with exultation. He got into his bunk as if in a dream. A feeling of profound peace, of pacific joy, came over him. On deck all was quiet.

Mr Massy, with his ear against the door of Jack's cabin, listened critically to a deep, stertorous breathing within. This was a dead-drunk sleep. The bout was over: tranquillized on that score, he, too, went in, and with slow wriggles got out of his old tweed jacket. It was a garment with many pockets, which he used to put on at odd times of the day, being subject to sudden chilly fits, and when he felt warmed he would take it off and hang it about anywhere all over the ship. It would be seen swinging on belaying-pins, thrown over the heads of winches, suspended on people's very door-handles for that matter. Was he not the owner? But his favourite place was a hook on a wooden awning stanchion on the bridge, almost against the binnacle. He had even in the early days more than one tussle on that point with Captain Whalley, who desired the bridge to be kept tidy. He had been overawed then. Of late, though, he had been able to defy his partner with impunity. Captain Whalley never seemed to notice anything. As to the Malays, in their awe of that scowling man not one of the crew would dream of laying a hand on the thing, no matter where or what it swung from.

With an unexpectedness which made Mr Massy jump and drop the coat at his feet, there came from the next berth the crash and thud of a headlong, jingling, clattering fall. The faithful Jack must have dropped to sleep suddenly as he sat at his revels, and now had gone over chair and all, breaking, as it seemed by the sound, every single glass and bottle in the place. After the terrific smash all was still for a time in there, as though he had killed himself on the spot. Mr Massy held his breath. At last a sleepy, uneasy groaning sigh was exhaled slowly on the other side of the bulkhead.

'I hope to goodness he's too drunk to wake up now,' muttered Mr Massy.

The sound of a softly knowing laugh nearly drove him to despair. He swore violently under his breath. The fool would keep him awake all night now for certain. He cursed his luck. He wanted to forget his maddening troubles in sleep sometimes. He could detect no movements. Without apparently making the slightest attempt to get up, Jack went on sniggering to himself where he lay; then began to speak, where he had left off as it were –

'Massy! I love the dirty rascal. He would like to see his poor old Jack starve – but just you look where he has climbed to ...' He hiccoughed in a superior, leisurely manner ... 'Shipowning it with the best. A lottery ticket you want. Ha! ha! I will give you lottery tickets, my boy. Let the old ship sink and the old chum starve – that's right. He don't go wrong – Massy don't. Not he. He's a genius – that man is. That's the way to win your money. Ship and chum must go.'

'The silly old fool has taken it to heart,' muttered Massy to himself. And, listening with a softened expression of face for any slight sign of returning drowsiness, he was discouraged profoundly by a burst of laughter full of joyful irony.

'Would like to see her at the bottom of the sea! Oh, you clever, clever devil! Wish her sunk, eh? I should think you would, my boy; the damned old thing and all your troubles with her. Rake in the insurance money – turn your back on your old chum – all's well – gentleman again.'

A grim stillness had come over Massy's face. Only his big eyes rolled uneasily. The raving fool. And yet it was all true. Yes. Lottery tickets, too. All true. What? Beginning again? He wished he wouldn't . . .

But it was even so. The imaginative drunkard on the other side of the bulkhead shook off the deathlike stillness that after his last words had fallen on the dark ship moored to a silent shore.

'Don't you dare to say anything against George Massy, Esquire. When he's tired of waiting he will do away with her. Look out! Down she goes – chum and all. He'll know how to . . .'

The voice hesitated, weary, dreamy, lost, as if dying away in a vast open space.

'. . . Find a trick that will work. He's up to it – never fear . . .'

He must have been very drunk, for at last the heavy sleep gripped him with the suddenness of a magic spell, and the last word lengthened itself into an interminable, noisy, indrawn snore. And then even the snoring stopped, and all was still.

But it seemed as though Mr Massy had suddenly come to doubt the efficacy of sleep as against a man's troubles; or perhaps he had found the relief he needed in the stillness of a calm contemplation that may contain the vivid thoughts of wealth, of a stroke of luck, of long idleness, and may bring before you the imagined form of every desire; for, turning about and throwing his arms over the edge of his bunk, he stood there with his feet on his favourite old coat, looking out through the round port into the night over the river. Sometimes a breath of wind would enter and touch his face, a cool breath charged with the damp, fresh feel from a vast body of water. A glimmer here and there was all he could see of it; and once he might after all suppose he had dozed off, since there appeared before his vision, unexpectedly and connected with no dream, a row of flaming and gigantic figures — three nought seven one two — making up a number such as you may see on a lottery ticket. And then all at once the port was no longer black: it was pearly grey, framing a shore crowded with houses, thatched roof beyond thatched roof, walls of mats and bamboo, gables of carved teak timber. Rows of dwellings raised on a forest of piles lined the steely bank of the river, brimful and still, with the tide on the turn. This was Batu Beru — and the day had come.

Mr Massy shook himself, put on the tweed coat, and, shivering nervously as if from some great shock, made a note of the number. A fortunate, rare hint that. Yes; but to pursue fortune one wanted money — ready cash.

Then he went out and prepared to descend into the engine-room. Several small jobs had to be seen to, and Jack was lying dead drunk on the floor of his cabin, with the door locked at that. His gorge rose at the thoughts of work. Ay! But if you wanted to do nothing you had to get first a good bit of money. A ship won't save you. True, all true. He was tired of waiting for some chance that would rid him at last of that ship that had turned out a curse on his life.

14

The deep, interminable hoot of the steam-whistle had, in its grave, vibrating note, something intolerable, which sent a slight shudder down Mr Van Wyk's back. It was the early afternoon; the *Sofala* was leaving Batu Beru for Pangu, the next place of call. She swung in the stream, scantily attended by a few canoes, and, gliding on the broad river, became lost to view from the Van Wyk bungalow.

Its owner had not gone this time to see her off. Generally he came down to the wharf, exchanged a few words with the bridge while she cast off, and waved his hand to Captain Whalley at the last moment. This day he did not even go as far as the balustrade of the verandah. 'He couldn't see me if I did,' he said to himself. 'I wonder whether he can make out the house at all.' And this thought somehow made him feel more alone than he had ever felt for all these years. What was it? six or seven? Seven. A long time.

He sat on the verandah with a closed book on his knee, and, as it were, looked out upon his solitude, as if the fact of Captain Whalley's blindness had opened his eyes to his own. There were many sorts of heartaches and troubles, and there was no place where they could not find a man out. And he felt ashamed, as though he had for six years behaved like a peevish boy.

His thought followed the *Sofala* on her way. On the spur of the moment he had acted impulsively, turning to the thing most pressing. And what else could he have done? Later on he should see. It seemed necessary that he should come out into the world, for a time at least. He had money – something could be arranged; he would grudge no time, no trouble, no loss of his solitude. It weighed on him now – and Captain Whalley appeared to him as he had sat shading his eyes, as if, being deceived in the trust of his faith, he were beyond all the good and evil that can be wrought by the hands of men.

Mr Van Wyk's thoughts followed the *Sofala* down the river, winding about through the belt of the coast forest, between the buttressed shafts of the big trees, through the mangrove strip, and over the bar. The ship crossed it easily in broad daylight, piloted, as it happened, by Mr Sterne, who took the watch from four to six, and then went below to hug himself with delight at the prospect of being virtually employed by a rich man – like Mr Van Wyk. He could not see how any hitch could occur now. He did not seem able to get over the feeling of being 'fixed up at last'. From six to eight, in the course of duty, the Serang looked alone after the ship. She had a clear road before her now till about three in the morning, when she would close with the Pangu group. At eight Mr Sterne came out cheerily to take charge again till midnight. At ten he was still chirruping and humming to himself on the bridge, and about that time Mr Van Wyk's thought abandoned the *Sofala*. Mr Van Wyk had fallen asleep at last.

Massy, blocking the engine-room companion, jerked himself into his tweed jacket surlily, while the second waited with a scowl.

'Oh. You came out! You sot! Well, what have you got to say for yourself?'

He had been in charge of the engines till then. A sombre fury darkened his mind: a hot anger against the ship, against the facts of life, against the men for their cheating, against himself, too – because of an inward tremor in his heart.

An incomprehensible growl answered him.

'What? Can't you open your mouth now? You yelp out your infernal rot loud enough when you are drunk. What do you mean by abusing people in that way? – you old useless boozer, you!'

'Can't help it. Don't remember anything about it. You shouldn't listen.'

'You dare to tell me! What do you mean by going on a drunk like this?'

'Don't ask me. Sick of the dam' boilers – you would be. Sick of Life.'

'I wish you were dead, then. You've made me sick of you. Don't you remember the uproar you made last night? You miserable old soaker!'

'No; I don't. Don't want to. Drink is drink.'

'I wonder what prevents me from kicking you out. What do you want here?'

'Relieve you. You've been long enough down there, George.'

'Don't you George me – you tippling old rascal, you! If I were to die tomorrow you would starve. Remember that. Say Mr Massy.'

'Mr Massy,' repeated the other, stolidly.

Dishevelled, with dull blood-shot eyes, a snuffy, grimy shirt, greasy trousers, naked feet thrust into ragged slippers, he bolted in head down directly Massy had made way for him.

The chief engineer looked around. The deck was empty as far as the taffrail. All the native passengers had left in Batu Beru this time, and no others had joined. The dial of the patent log tinkled periodically in the dark at the end of the ship. It was a dead calm, and, under the clouded sky, through the still air that seemed to cling warm, with a seaweed smell, to her slim hull, on a sea of sombre grey and unwrinkled, the ship moved on an even keel, as if floating detached in empty space. But Mr

Massy slapped his forehead, tottered a little, and caught hold of a belaying-pin at the foot of the mast.

'I shall go mad,' he muttered, walking across the deck unsteadily. A shovel was scraping loose coal down below – a fire-door clanged. Sterne on the bridge began whistling a new tune.

Captain Whalley, sitting on the couch, awake and fully dressed, heard the door of his cabin open. He did not move in the least, waiting to recognize the voice, with an appalling strain of prudence.

A bulkhead lamp blazed on the white paint, the crimson plush, the brown varnish of mahogany tops. The white wood packing-case under the bed-place had remained unopened for three years now, as though Captain Whalley had felt that, after the *Fair Maid* was gone, there could be no abiding-place on earth for his affections. His hands rested on his knees; his handsome head with big eyebrows presented a rigid profile to the doorway. The expected voice spoke out at last.

'Once more, then. What am I to call you?'

Ha! Massy. Again. The weariness of it crushed his heart – and the pain of shame was almost more than he could bear without crying out.

'Well. Is it to be "partner" still?'

'You don't know what you ask.'

'I know what I want . . .'

Massy stepped in and closed the door.

'. . . And I am going to have a try for it with you once more.'

His whine was half persuasive, half menacing.

'For it's no manner of use to tell me that you are poor. You don't spend anything on yourself, that's true enough; but there's another name for that. You think you are going to have what you want out of me for three years, and then cast me off without hearing what I think of you. You think I would have submitted to your airs if I had known you had only a beggarly five hundred pounds in the world. You ought to have told me.'

'Perhaps,' said Captain Whalley, bowing his head. 'And yet it has saved you . . .' Massy laughed scornfully . . . 'I have told you often enough since.'

'And I don't believe you now. When I think how I let you

lord it over my ship! Do you remember how you used to bully-rag me about my coat and *your* bridge? It was in his way. *His* bridge! "And I won't be a party to this – and I couldn't think of doing that." Honest man! And now it all comes out. "I am poor, and I can't. I have only this five hundred in the world." '

He contemplated the immobility of Captain Whalley, that seemed to present an inconquerable obstacle in his path. His face took a mournful cast.

'You are a hard man.'

'Enough,' said Captain Whalley, turning upon him. 'You shall get nothing from me, because I have nothing of mine to give away now.'

'Tell that to the marines!'

Mr Massy, going out, looked back once; then the door closed, and Captain Whalley, alone, sat as still as before. He had nothing of his own – even his own past of honour, of truth, of just pride, was gone. All his spotless life had fallen into the abyss. He had said his last good-bye to it. But what belonged to *her*, that he meant to save. Only a little money. He would take it to her in his own hands – this last gift of a man that had lasted too long. And an immense and fierce impulse, the very passion of paternity, flamed up with all the unquenched vigour of his worthless life in a desire to see her face.

Just across the deck Massy had gone straight to his cabin, struck a light, and hunted up the note of the dreamed number whose figures had flamed up also with the fierceness of another passion. He must contrive somehow not to miss a drawing. That number meant something. But what expedient could he contrive to keep himself going?

'Wretched miser!' he mumbled.

If Mr Sterne could at no time have told him anything new about his partner, he could have told Mr Sterne that another use could be made of a man's affliction than just to kick him out, and thus defer the term of a difficult payment for a year. To keep the secret of the affliction and induce him to stay was a better move. If without means, he would be anxious to remain; and that settled the question of refunding him his share. He did not know exactly how much Captain Whalley was disabled; but if it so happened that he put the ship ashore somewhere for good and all, it was not the owner's fault – was it? He was not obliged to know that there was anything wrong. But probably nobody would raise such a point, and the ship was fully insured. He had had enough self-restraint to pay up the premiums. But this was not all. He could not believe Captain Whalley to be so confoundedly destitute as not to have some more money put away somewhere. If he, Massy, could get hold of it, that would pay for the boilers, and everything went on as before. And if she got lost in the end, so much the better. He hated her: he loathed the troubles that took his mind off the chances of fortune. He wished her at the bottom of the sea, and the insurance money in his pocket. And as, baffled, he left Captain Whalley's cabin, he enveloped in the same hatred the ship with the worn-out boilers and the man with the dimmed eyes.

And our conduct after all is so much a matter of outside suggestion, that had it not been for his Jack's drunken gabble he would have there and then had it out with this miserable man, who would neither help, nor stay, nor yet lose the ship. The old fraud! He longed to kick him out. But he restrained himself. Time enough for that – when he liked. There was a fearful new thought put into his head. Wasn't he up to it after all? How that beast Jack had raved! 'Find a safe trick to get rid of her.' Well, Jack was not so far wrong. A very clever trick had occurred to him. Ay! But what of the risk?

A feeling of pride – the pride of superiority to common prejudices – crept into his breast, made his heart beat fast, his mouth turn dry. Not everybody would dare; but he was Massy, and he was up to it!

Six bells were struck on deck. Eleven! He drank a glass of water, and sat down for ten minutes or so to calm himself. Then he got out of his chest a small bull's-eye lantern of his own and lit it.

Almost opposite his berth, across the narrow passage under the bridge, there was, in the iron deck-structure covering the stokehold fiddle and the boiler-space, a storeroom with iron sides, iron roof, iron-plated floor, too, on account of the heat below. All sorts of rubbish was shot there: it had a mound of scrap-iron in a corner; rows of empty oil-cans; sacks of cotton-waste, with a heap of charcoal, a deck-forge, fragments of an old hen-coop, winch-covers all in rags, remnants of lamps, and a brown felt hat, discarded by a man dead now (of a fever on the Brazil coast), who had been once mate of the *Sofala*, had remained for years jammed forcibly behind a length of burst copper pipe, flung at some time or other out of the engine-room. A complete and impervious blackness pervaded that Capharnaum of forgotten things. A small shaft of light from Mr Massy's bull's-eye fell slanting right through it.

His coat was unbuttoned; he shot the bolt of the door (there was no other opening), and, squatting before the scrap-heap, began to pack his pockets with pieces of iron. He packed them carefully, as if the rusty nuts, the broken bolts, the links of cargo chain, had been so much gold he had that one chance to carry away. He packed his side-pockets till they bulged, the breast-pocket, the pockets inside. He turned over the pieces. Some he rejected. A small mist of powdered rust began to rise about his busy hands. Mr Massy knew something of the scientific basis of his clever trick. If you want to deflect the magnetic needle of a ship's compass, soft iron is the best; likewise many small pieces in the pockets of a jacket would have more effect than a few large ones, because in that way you obtain a greater amount of surface for weight in your iron, and it's surface that tells.

He slipped out swiftly – two strides sufficed – and in his cabin he perceived that his hands were all red – red with rust. It disconcerted him, as though he had found them covered with blood: he looked himself over hastily. Why, his trousers, too! He had been rubbing his rusty palms on his legs.

He tore off the waistband button in his haste, brushed his coat, washed his hands. Then the air of guilt left him, and he sat down to wait.

He sat bolt upright and weighted with iron in his chair. He had a hard, lumpy bulk against each hip, felt the scrappy iron in his pockets touch his ribs at every breath, the downward drag of all these pounds hanging upon his shoulders. He looked very dull, too, sitting idle there, and his yellow face, with motionless black eyes, had something passive and sad in its quietness.

When he heard eight bells struck above his head, he rose and made ready to go out. His movements seemed aimless, his lower lip had dropped a little, his eyes roamed about the cabin, and the tremendous tension of his will had robbed them of every vestige of intelligence.

With the last stroke of the bell the Serang appeared noiselessly on the bridge to relieve the mate. Sterne overflowed with good nature, since he had nothing more to desire.

'Got your eyes well open yet, Serang? It's middling dark; I'll wait till you get your sight properly.'

The old Malay murmured, looked up with his worn eyes, sidled away into the light of the binnacle, and, clasping his hands behind his back, fixed his eyes on the compass-card.

'You'll have to keep a good lookout ahead for land, about half-past three. It's fairly clear, though. You have looked in on the captain as you came along – eh? He knows the time? Well, then, I am off.'

At the foot of the ladder he stood aside for the captain. He watched him go up with an even, certain tread, and remained thoughtful for a moment. 'It's funny,' he said to himself, 'but you can never tell whether that man has seen you or not. He might have heard me breathe this time.'

He was a wonderful man when all was said and done. They said he had had a name in his day. Mr Sterne could well believe it; and he concluded serenely that Captain Whalley must be able to see people more or less – as himself just now, for instance – but not being certain of anybody, had to keep up that unnoticing silence of manner for fear of giving himself away. Mr Sterne was a shrewd guesser.

This necessity of every moment brought home to Captain Whalley's heart the humiliation of his falsehood. He had drifted into it from paternal love, from incredulity, from boundless trust in divine justice meted out to men's feelings on this earth. He would give his poor Ivy the benefit of another month's work; perhaps the affliction was only temporary. Surely God would not rob his child of his power to help, and cast him naked into a night without end. He had caught at every hope; and when the evidence of his misfortune was stronger than hope, he tried not to believe the manifest thing.

In vain. In the steadily darkening universe a sinister clearness fell upon his ideas. In the illuminating moments of suffering he saw life, men, all things, the whole earth with all her burden of created nature, as he had never seen them before.

Sometimes he was seized with a sudden vertigo and an overwhelming terror; and then the image of his daughter appeared. Her, too, he had never seen so clearly before. Was it possible that he should ever be unable to do anything whatever for her? Nothing. And not see her any more? Never.

Why? The punishment was too great for a little presumption, for a little pride. And at last he came to cling to his deception with a fierce determination to carry it out to the end, to save her money intact, and behold her once more with his own eyes. Afterwards – what? The idea of suicide was revolting to the vigour of his manhood. He had prayed for death till the prayers had stuck in his throat. All the days of his life he had prayed, for daily bread, and not to be led into temptation, in a childlike humility of spirit. Did words mean anything? Whence did the gift of speech come? The violent beating of his heart reverberated in his head – seemed to shake his brain to pieces.

He sat down heavily in the deck-chair to keep the pretence of his watch. The night was dark. All the nights were dark now.

'Serang,' he said, half aloud.

'Ada, Tuan. I am here.'

'There are clouds on the sky?'

'There are, Tuan.'

'Let her be steered straight. North.'

'She is going north, Tuan.'

The Serang stepped back. Captain Whalley recognized Massy's footfalls on the bridge.

The engineer walked over to port and returned, passing behind the chair several times. Captain Whalley detected an unusual character as of prudent care in this prowling. The near presence of that man brought with it always a recrudescence of moral suffering for Captain Whalley. It was not remorse. After all, he had done nothing but good to the poor devil. There was also a sense of danger – the necessity of a greater care.

Massy stopped and said –

'So you still say you must go?'

'I must indeed.'

'And you couldn't at least leave the money for a term of years?'

'Impossible.'

'Can't trust it with me without your care, eh?'

Captain Whalley remained silent. Massy sighed deeply over the back of the chair.

'It would just do to save me,' he said in a tremulous voice.

'I've saved you once.'

The chief engineer took off his coat with careful movements, and proceeded to feel for the brass hook screwed into the wooden stanchion. For this purpose he placed himself right in front of the binnacle, thus hiding completely the compass-card from the quartermaster at the wheel. 'Tuan!' the lascar at last murmured softly, meaning to let the white man know that he could not see to steer.

Mr Massy had accomplished his purpose. The coat was hanging from the nail, within six inches of the binnacle. And directly he had stepped aside the quartermaster, a middle-aged, pock-marked, Sumatra Malay, almost as dark as a negro, perceived with amazement that in that short time, in this smooth water, with no wind at all, the ship had gone swinging far out of her course. He had never known her get away like this before. With a slight grunt of astonishment he turned the wheel hastily to bring her head back north, which was the course. The grinding of the steering-chains, the chiding murmurs of the Serang, who had come over to the wheel, made a slight stir, which attracted Captain Whalley's anxious attention. He said, 'Take better care.' Then everything settled to the usual quiet on the bridge. Mr Massy had disappeared.

But the iron in the pockets of the coat had done its work; and the *Sofala*, heading north by the compass made untrue by this simple device, was no longer making a safe course for Pangu Bay.

The hiss of water parted by her stem, the throb of her engines, all the sounds of her faithful and laborious life, went on uninterrupted in the great calm of the sea joining on all sides the motionless layer of cloud over the sky. A gentle stillness as vast as the world seemed to wait upon her path, enveloping her lovingly in a supreme caress. Mr Massy thought there could be no better night for an arranged shipwreck.

Run up high and dry on one of the reefs east of Pangu – wait for daylight – hole in the bottom – out boats – Pangu Bay same evening. That's about it. As soon as she touched he would hasten on the bridge, get hold of the coat (nobody would notice in the dark), and shake it upside down over the side, or even fling it into the sea. A detail. Who could guess? Coat been seen hanging there from that hook hundreds of times. Nevertheless, when he sat down on the lower step of the bridge-ladder his knees knocked together a little. The waiting part was the worst of it. At times he would begin to pant quickly, as though he had been running, and then breathe largely, swelling with the intimate sense of a mastered fate. Now and then he would hear the shuffle of the Serang's bare feet up there: quiet, low voices would exchange a few words, and lapse almost at once into silence ...

'Tell me directly you see any land, Serang.'

'Yes, Tuan. Not yet.'

'No, not yet,' Captain Whalley would agree.

The ship had been the best friend of his decline. He had sent all the money he had made by and in the *Sofala* to his daughter. His thought lingered on the name. How often he and his wife had talked over the cot of the child in the big stern-cabin of the *Condor*; she would grow up, she would marry, she would love them, they would live near her and look at her happiness – it would go on without end. Well, his wife was dead, to the child he had given all he had to give; he wished he could come near her, see her, see her face once, live in the sound of her voice, that could make the darkness of the living grave ready for him supportable. He had been starved of love too long. He imagined her tenderness.

The Serang had been peering forward, and now and then glancing at the chair. He fidgeted restlessly, and suddenly burst out close to Captain Whalley –

'Tuan, do you see anything of the land?'

The alarmed voice brought Captain Whalley to his feet at once. He! See! And at the question, the curse of his blindness seemed to fall on him with a hundredfold force.

'What's the time?' he cried.

'Half-past three, Tuan.'

'We are close. You *must* see. Look, I say. Look.'

Mr Massy, awakened by the sudden sound of talking from a short doze on the lowest step, wondered why he was there. Ah! A faintness came over him. It is one thing to sow the seed of an accident and another to see the monstrous fruit hanging over your head ready to fall in the sound of agitated voice. 'There's no danger,' he muttered thickly to himself.

The horror of incertitude had seized upon Captain Whalley, the miserable mistrust of men, of things – of the very earth. He had steered that very course thirty-six times by the same compass – if anything was certain in this world it was its absolute, unerring correctness. Then what had happened? Did the Serang lie? Why lie? Why? Was he going blind, too?

'Is there a mist? Look low on the water. Low down, I say.'

'Tuan, there's no mist. See for yourself.'

Captain Whalley steadied the trembling of his limbs by an effort. Should he stop the engines at once and give himself away? A gust of irresolution swayed all sorts of bizarre notions in his mind. The unusual had come, and he was not fit to deal with it. In this passage of inexpressible anguish he saw her face – the face of a young girl – with an amazing strength of illusion. No, he must not give himself away after having gone so far for her sake. 'You steered the course? You made it? Speak the truth.'

'Ya, Tuan. On the course now. Look.'

Captain Whalley strode to the binnacle, which to him made such a dim spot of light in an infinity of shapeless shadow. By bending his face right down to the glass he had been able before ...

Having to stoop so low, he put out, instinctively, his arm to where he knew there was a stanchion to steady himself against. His hand closed on something that was not wood but cloth. The slight pull adding to the weight, the loop broke, and Mr Massy's coat falling, struck the deck heavily with a dull thump, accompanied by a lot of clicks.

'What's this?'

Captain Whalley fell on his knees, with groping hands extended in a frank gesture of blindness. They trembled, these hands feeling for the truth. He saw it. Iron near the compass. Wrong course. Wreck her! His ship. Oh, no. Not that.

'Jump and stop her!' he roared out in a voice not his own.

He ran himself – hands forward, a blind man, and while the clanging of the gong echoed still all over the ship, she seemed to butt full tilt into the side of a mountain.

It was low water along the north side of the strait. Mr Massy had not reckoned on that. Instead of running aground for half her length, the *Sofala* butted the sheer ridge of a stone reef which would have been awash at high water. This made the shock absolutely terrific. Everybody in the ship that was standing was thrown down headlong: the shaken rigging made a great rattling to the very trucks. All the lights went out; several chain-guys, snapping, clattered against the funnel; there were crashes, pings of parted wire-rope, splintering sounds, loud cracks; the masthead lamp flew over the bows, and all the doors about the deck began to bang heavily. Then, after having hit, she rebounded, hit the second time the very same spot like a battering-ram. This completed the havoc: the funnel, with all the guys gone, fell over with a hollow sound of thunder, smashing the wheel to bits, crushing the frame of the awnings, breaking the lockers, filling the bridge with a mass of broken wood. Captain Whalley picked himself up and stood knee-deep in wreckage, torn, bleeding, knowing the nature of the danger he had escaped mostly by the sound, and holding Mr Massy's coat in his arms.

By this time Sterne (he had been flung out of his bunk) had set the engines astern. They worked for a few turns, then a voice bawled out, 'Get out of the damned engine-room, Jack!' – and they stopped; but the ship had gone clear of the reef and lay still, with a heavy cloud of steam issuing from the broken deck-pipes, and vanishing in wispy shapes into the night. Notwithstanding the suddenness of the disaster there was no shouting, as if the very violence of the shock had half-stunned the shadowy lot of people swaying here and there about her decks. The voice of the Serang pronounced distinctly above the confused murmurs –

'No bottom.' He had heaved the lead.

Mr Sterne cried out next in a strained pitch –

'Where the devil has she got to? Where are we?'

Captain Whalley replied in a calm bass –

'Amongst the reefs to the eastward.'

'You know it, sir? Then she will never get out again.'

'She will be gone in five minutes. Boats, Sterne. Even one will save you all in this calm.'

The Chinaman stokers went in a disorderly rush for the port boats. Nobody tried to check them. The Malays, after a moment of confusion, became quiet, and Mr Sterne showed a good countenance. Captain Whalley had not moved. His thoughts were darker than this night in which he had lost his first ship.

'He made me lose a ship.'

Another tall figure standing before him amongst the litter of the smash on the bridge whispered insanely –

'Say nothing of it.'

Massy stumbled closer. Captain Whalley heard the chattering of his teeth.

'I have the coat.'

'Throw it down and come along,' urged the chattering voice. 'B-b-b-b-boat!'

'You will get five years for this.'

Mr Massy had lost his voice. His speech was a mere dry rustling in his throat.

'Have mercy!'

'Had you any when you made me lose my ship? Mr Massy, you shall get five years for this!'

'I wanted money! Money! My own money! I will give you some money. Take half of it. You love money yourself.'

'There's a justice . . .'

Massy made an awful effort, and in a strange, half-choked utterance –

'You blind devil! It's you that drove me to it.'

Captain Whalley, hugging the coat to his breast, made no sound. The light had ebbed for ever from the world – let everything go. But this man should not escape scot-free.

Sterne's voice commanded –

'Lower away!'

The blocks rattled.

'Now then,' he cried, 'over with you. This way. You, Jack, here. Mr Massy! Mr Massy! Captain! Quick, sir! Let's get –'

'I shall go to prison for trying to cheat the insurance, but you'll get exposed; you, honest man, who has been cheating me. You are poor. Aren't you? You've nothing but the five hundred pounds. Well, you have nothing at all now. The ship's lost, and the insurance won't be paid.'

Captain Whalley did not move. True! Ivy's money. Gone in this wreck. Again he had a flash of insight. He was indeed at the end of his tether.

Urgent voices cried out together alongside. Massy did not seem able to tear himself away from the bridge. He chattered and hissed despairingly –

'Give it up to me! Give it up!'

'No,' said Captain Whalley; 'I could not give it up. You had better go. Don't wait, man, if you want to live. She's settling down by the head fast. No; I shall keep it, but I shall stay on board.'

Massy did not seem to understand; but the love of life, awakened suddenly, drove him away from the bridge.

Captain Whalley laid the coat down, and stumbled amongst the heaps of wreckage to the side.

'Is Mr Massy with you?' he called out into the night.

Sterne from the boat shouted –

'Yes; we've got him. Come along, sir. It's madness to stay longer.'

Captain Whalley felt along the rail carefully, and, without a word, cast off the painter. They were expecting him still down there. They were waiting, till a voice suddenly exclaimed –

'We are adrift! Shove off!'

'Captain Whalley! Leap! ... pull up a little ... leap! You can swim.'

In that old heart, in that vigorous body, there was, that nothing should be wanting, a horror of death that apparently could not be overcome by the horror of blindness. But after all, for Ivy he had carried his point, walking in his darkness to the very verge of a crime. God had not listened to his prayers. The light had finished ebbing out of the world; not a glimmer. It was a dark waste; but it was unseemly that a Whalley who had gone so far to carry a point should continue to live. He must pay the price.

'Leap as far as you can, sir; we will pick you up.'

They did not hear him answer. But their shouting seemed to remind him of something. He groped his way back, and sought for Mr Massy's coat. He could swim indeed; people sucked down by the whirlpool of a sinking ship do come up sometimes to the surface, and it was unseemly that a Whalley, who had made up his mind to die, should be beguiled by chance into a struggle. He would put all these pieces of iron into his own pockets.

They, looking from the boat, saw the *Sofala*, a black mass upon a black sea, lying at an appalling cant. No sound came from her. Then, with a great bizarre shuffling noise, as if the boilers had broken through the bulkheads, and with a faint muffled detonation, where the ship had been there appeared for a moment something standing upright and narrow, like a rock out of the sea. Then that, too, disappeared.

When the *Sofala* failed to come back to Batu Beru at the proper time, Mr Van Wyk understood at once that he would never see her any more. But he did not know what had happened till some weeks afterwards, when, in a native craft lent him by his Sultan, he had made his way to the *Sofala*'s port of registry, where already her existence and the official inquiry into her loss were beginning to be forgotten.

It had not been a very remarkable or interesting case, except for the fact that the captain had gone down with his sinking ship. It was the only life lost; and Mr Van Wyk would not have been able to learn any details had it not been for Sterne, whom he met one day on the quay near the bridge over the creek, almost on the very spot where Captain Whalley, to preserve his daughter's five hundred pounds intact, had turned to get a sampan which would take him on board the *Sofala*.

From afar Mr Van Wyk saw Sterne blink straight at him and raise his hand to his hat. They drew into the shade of a building (it was a bank), and the mate related how the boats with the crew got into Pangu Bay about six hours after the accident, and how they had lived for a fortnight in a state of destitution before they found an opportunity to get away from that beastly place. The inquiry had exonerated everybody from all blame. The loss of the ship was put down to an unusual set of the current. Indeed, it could not have been anything else: there was no other way to account for the ship being set seven miles to the eastward of her position during the middle watch.

'A piece of bad luck for me, sir.'

Sterne passed his tongue on his lips and glanced aside. 'I lost the advantage of being employed by you, sir. I can never be sorry enough. But here it is: one man's poison, another man's meat. This could not have been handier for Mr Massy if he had arranged that shipwreck himself. The most timely loss I've ever heard of.'

'What became of that Massy?' asked Mr Van Wyk.

'He, sir? Ha! ha! He would keep on telling me that he meant to buy another ship; but as soon as he had the money in his pocket he cleared out for Manila by mail-boat early in the morning. I gave him chase right aboard, and he told me then he was going to make his fortune dead sure in Manila. I could go to the devil for all he cared. And yet he as good as promised to give me the command if I didn't talk too much.'

'You never said anything . . .' Mr Van Wyk began.

'Not I, sir. Why should I? I mean to get on, but the dead aren't in my way,' said Sterne. His eyelids were beating rapidly, then drooped for an instant. 'Besides, sir, it would have been an awkward business. You made me hold my tongue just a bit too long.'

'Do you know how it was that Captain Whalley remained on board? Did he really refuse to leave? Come now! Or was it perhaps an accidental . . .?'

'Nothing!' Sterne interrupted with energy. 'I tell you I yelled for him to leap overboard. He simply *must* have cast off the painter of the boat himself. We all yelled to him – that is, Jack and I. He wouldn't even answer us. The ship was as silent as a grave to the last. Then the boilers fetched away, and down she went. Accident! Not it! The game was up, sir, I tell you.'

This was all that Sterne had to say.

Mr Van Wyk had been of course made the guest of the club for a fortnight, and it was there that he met the lawyer in whose office had been signed the agreement between Massy and Captain Whalley.

'Extraordinary old man,' he said. 'He came into my office

from nowhere in particular as you may say, with his five hundred pounds to invest, and that engineer fellow following him anxiously. And now he is gone out a little inexplicably, just as he came. I could never understand him quite. There was no mystery at all about that Massy, eh? I wonder whether Whalley refused to leave the ship. It would have been foolish. He was blameless, as the court found.'

Mr Van Wyk had known him well, he said, and he could not believe in suicide. Such an act would not have been in character with what he knew of the man.

'It is my opinion, too,' the lawyer agreed. The general theory was that the captain had remained too long on board trying to save something of importance. Perhaps the chart which would clear him, or else something of value in his cabin. The painter of the boat had come adrift of itself, it was supposed. However, strange to say, some little time before that voyage poor Whalley had called in his office and had left with him a sealed envelope addressed to his daughter, to be forwarded to her in case of his death. Still it was nothing very unusual, especially in a man of his age. Mr Van Wyk shook his head. Captain Whalley looked good for a hundred years.

'Perfectly true,' assented the lawyer. 'The old fellow looked as though he had come into the world full grown and with that long beard. I could never, somehow, imagine him either younger or older – don't you know. There was a sense of physical power about that man, too. And perhaps that was the secret of that something peculiar in his person which struck everybody who came in contact with him. He looked indestructible by any ordinary means that put an end to the rest of us. His deliberate, stately courtesy of manner was full of significance. It was as though he were certain of having plenty of time for everything. Yes, there was something indestructible about him; and the way he talked sometimes you might have thought he believed it himself. When he called on me last with that letter he wanted me to take charge of, he was not depressed at all. Perhaps a shade more deliberate in his talk and manner. Not depressed in the least. Had he a presentiment, I wonder? Perhaps! Still it seems a miserable end for such a striking figure.'

'Oh, yes! It was a miserable end,' Mr Van Wyk said, with so

much fervour that the lawyer looked up at him curiously; and afterwards, after parting with him, he remarked to an acquaintance –

'Queer person that Dutch tobacco-planter from Batu Beru. Know anything of him?'

'Heaps of money,' answered the bank manager. 'I hear he's going home by the next mail to form a company to take over his estates. Another tobacco district thrown open. He's wise, I think. These good times won't last for ever.'

In the southern hemisphere Captain Whalley's daughter had no presentiment of evil when she opened the envelope addressed to her in the lawyer's handwriting. She had received it in the afternoon; all the boarders had gone out, her boys were at school, her husband sat upstairs in his big arm-chair with a book, thin-faced, wrapped up in rugs to the waist. The house was still, and the greyness of a cloudy day lay against the panes of the windows. In the shabby dining-room, where a faint cold smell of dishes lingered all the year round, sitting at the end of a long table surrounded by many chairs pushed in with their backs close against the edge of the perpetually laid table-cloth, she read the opening sentences: 'Most profound regret – painful duty – your father is no more – in accordance with his instructions – fatal casualty – consolation – no blame to his memory . . .'

Her face was thin, her temples a little sunk under the smoother bands of black hair, her lips remained resolutely compressed, while her dark eyes grew larger, till at last, with a low cry, she stood up, and instantly stooped to pick up another envelope which had slipped off her knees on to the floor.

She tore it open, snatched out the enclosure . . .

'My dearest child,' it said, 'I am writing this while I am able yet to write legibly. I am trying hard to save for you all the money that is left; I have only kept it to serve you better. It is yours. It shall not be lost; it shall not be touched. There's five hundred pounds. Of what I have earned I have kept nothing back till now. For the future, if I live, I must keep back some – a little – to bring me to you. I must come to you. I must see you once more.

'It is hard to believe that you will ever look on these lines.

God seems to have forgotten me. I want to see you – and yet death would be a greater favour. If you ever read these words, I charge you to begin by thanking a God merciful at last, for I shall be dead then, and it will be well. My dear, I am at the end of my tether.'

The next paragraph began with the words: 'My sight is going ...'

She read no more that day. The hand holding up the paper to her eyes fell slowly, and her slender figure in a plain black dress walked rigidly to the window. Her eyes were dry: no cry of sorrow or whisper of thanks went up to heaven from her lips. Life had been too hard, for all the efforts of his love. It had silenced her emotions. But for the first time in all these years its sting had departed, the carking care of poverty, the meanness of a hard struggle for bread. Even the image of her husband and of her children seemed to glide away from her into the grey twilight; it was her father's face alone that she saw, as though he had come to see her, always quiet and big, as she had seen him last, but with something more august and tender in his aspect.

She slipped his folded letter between the two buttons of her plain black bodice, and leaning her forehead against a window-pane remained there till dusk, perfectly motionless, giving him all the time she could spare. Gone! Was it possible? My God, was it possible? The blow had come softened by the spaces of the earth, by the years of absence. There had been whole days when she had not thought of him at all – had no time. But she had loved him, she felt she had loved him after all.

MORE ABOUT PENGUINS
AND PELICANS

Penguinews, which appears every month, contains details of all the new books issued by Penguins as they are published. From time to time it is supplemented by *Penguins in Print*, which is our complete list of almost 5,000 titles.

A specimen copy of *Penguinews* will be sent to you free on request. Please write to Dept EP, Penguin Books Ltd, Harmondsworth, Middlesex, for your copy.

In the U.S.A.: For a complete list of books available from Penguins in the United States write to Dept CS, Penguin Books, 625 Madison Avenue, New York, New York 10022.

In Canada: For a complete list of books available from Penguins in Canada write to Penguin Books Canada Ltd, 2801 John Street, Markham, Ontario L3R 1B4.

Arnold Bennett

THE CLAYHANGER TRILOGY

CLAYHANGER *

Arnold Bennett's careful evocation of a boy growing to manhood during the last quarter of the nineteenth century, with its superb portrait of an autocratic father, stands on a literary level with *The Old Wives' Tale*.

HILDA LESSWAYS *

Relating the early life of Hilda Lessways, before her marriage to Edwin Clayhanger. Her involvement with the enigmatic, self-made man, George Cannon, and his enterprises take her from the offices of an embryo newspaper in the Five Towns to a venture into the guest house business in Brighton.

THESE TWAIN *

In what is in many ways the most accomplished novel of the trilogy, Bennett achieves a remarkably subtle and biting portrait of a marriage. Hilda and Edwin Clayhanger are living in Bursley, with Hilda's son by her disastrous 'marriage' to George Cannon. As they cope with immediate tensions and old wounds, they are forced continually to reassess their relationship.

Also published in Penguins

ANNA OF THE FIVE TOWNS

THE CARD

THE GRAND BABYLON HOTEL *

THE GRIM SMILE OF THE FIVE TOWNS

and

THE JOURNALS

* ALSO PUBLISHED IN PENGUINS IN THE U.S.A.

JOSEPH CONRAD

'Conrad is among the very greatest novelists in the language – or any language' – F. R. Leavis in *The Great Tradition*

Seven other books by Conrad are now available in Penguins:

LORD JIM *

The novel by which Conrad is most often remembered by perhaps a majority of readers, and the first considerable novel he wrote.

THE SECRET AGENT: *A Simple Tale*

Based on anarchist and terrorist activities in London, this novel has been described by Dr Leavis as 'indubitably a classic and a masterpiece'.

VICTORY: *An Island Tale*

In his critical biography of the author, Jocelyn Baines places this tragic story of the Malay Archipelago 'among Conrad's best novels'.

THE NIGGER OF THE NARCISSUS, TYPHOON *
and Other Stories

Conrad's first sea novel, together with 'Typhoon', 'Falk', 'Amy Foster', and 'Tomorrow'.

NOSTROMO: *A Tale of the Seaboard* *

His story of revolution in South America, which Arnold Bennett regarded 'as one of the greatest novels of any age'.

HEART OF DARKNESS *

T. S. Eliot's use of a quotation from *Heart of Darkness* as an epigraph to the original manuscript of *The Waste Land* was no doubt inspired by his belief that Mr Kurtz, the ambiguous hero of the story, stands at the dark heart of the twentieth century.

* ALSO PUBLISHED IN PENGUINS IN THE U.S.A.